Arizona Mayhem

Forder managed to get into a sitting position. He was half-turned away from Carter. His right hand was sliding inside his jacket, reaching into his left armpit. Carter watched him until the hand reappeared from the jacket, saw it was holding a gun, and lunged forward to grapple with him.

While Carter was concentrating on Forder, Cassie produced a .41 derringer from under a cloth on the table and turned on him, her face contorted with desperation. She fired the weapon. The crash of the shot filled the small room with gun thunder. Carter felt the impact of the slug as if he had been struck by lightning. Pain lanced through him, although, momentarily, he had no idea where he had been hit.

His sense of balance fled, and he became aware that the floor was coming up to hit him in the face. At the impact, he lost consciousness. . . .

Arizona Mayhem

Corba Sunman

A Black Horse Western

ROBERT HALE

© Corba Sunman 2018
First published in Great Britain 2018

ISBN 978-0-7198-2766-2

The Crowood Press
The Stable Block
Crowood Lane
Ramsbury
Marlborough
Wiltshire SN8 2HR

www.bhwesterns.com

Robert Hale is an imprint
of The Crowood Press

ONE

Link Carter came out of the hills west of Singletree, Arizona, and reined in when he saw the cluster of buildings before him. He had endured three months of travelling since turning his back on his previous life and career in the Texas Rangers. He had reached a crossroads back in Texas, and now he was seeking his brother Nick, three years his junior, who was rumoured to be in business on the Singletree range. He hoped to settle down with Nick, make a place for himself, and start a new life that was peaceful and non-violent.

He stretched his long body gingerly, trying to release the ache of travel in his bones. A nagging strand of worry had been clawing along his spine for the last ten miles, and he was keenly aware of his back trail, for he had seen signs of pursuit at the Texas border and that he had left some unfinished business back there. But he seemed to have shaken off the two men who had started following him and tried to dismiss them from his mind.

He touched spurs to his grey and started down a long slope to the single street, intent now on starting his new venture. He was tall in the saddle, big-boned and well-muscled, his hard face showing the signs and stresses of his previous violent life. His blue eyes were narrowed, and deep-set, far-seeing, and fair hair showed from beneath his Stetson. His mouth was a mere slit under a small nose. He was wearing a green check shirt and black pants, and a cartridge belt circled his waist, with a holster on his right hip containing a Colt .45 pistol. A saddle scabbard under his right thigh held a Winchester 40.40 carbine. Behind his saddle he carried his bedroll and the necessities of life required for travelling long distances through the wilderness.

The grey moved forward instantly at the touch of his spurs, and before the horse could take more than one step a bullet crackled by Carter's left ear. The report of a rifle sounded in the background. He moved without thought, diving to his left, kicking his feet from the stirrups. As he left the saddle in a flying leap his right hand dropped to the butt of the Winchester and it slid smoothly from its saddle boot as he fell to the ground.

Several shots hammered, and he heard slugs plunking around him. He hit the ground hard and rolled a couple of yards before coming up into the aim, his keen gaze seeking to pinpoint the trouble. He could hear the deeper sound of a Colt booming in the background, coming from a different angle than the Winchester. The volume of flying lead made him duck, and he waited for a respite in the shooting before raising himself to observe. He saw a rider pounding towards his position, waving a pistol, yelling like a Confederate cavalryman charging the Union positions at Shiloh, and spotted drifting gun smoke from another direction, where a motionless figure was handling a long gun.

Carter lifted his rifle, sent two quick shots at the rider, and when the animal went down in a heap of threshing hoofs he turned his attention to the man with the rifle. A 40.40 slug crackled by his Stetson, and he replied instantly, triggering two shots at the exposed head and right shoulder of his target. The man slumped, and Carter saw the rifle fly out of his grasp.

The shooting ceased abruptly, and echoes drifted away across the range. Carter wiped sweat from his face with a dusty sleeve. The rider was gone from the crumpled horse, and he looked around for signs of him. A pistol hammered, and a slug whined over Carter's head. He went to cover and waited.

'I got you dead to rights, Carter. We trailed you all the way from Texas. You killed my brother Jack and my Uncle Ben before you left, and I want to spill your blood. Come on out into the open and fight me man to man.

'You know you ain't got a hope in hell of beating me from an even break. I'm Billy Warner on the

7

blood trail, and I'm gonna put you six feet under.'

'Billy, you couldn't bury a jack rabbit if it was half dead. Stick your head out of cover and I'll put you out of your misery.'

Warner triggered his Colt, emptying it in his fury. Carter slid out of his cover, gun levelled. He saw Warner crouching, reloading his cylinder, and went forward silently, watching his man intently. Warner finished reloading and closed his gun. He looked up, and when he saw Carter out in the open he flipped his pistol into the aim. Carter squeezed his trigger. His gun recoiled in his hand and smoke drifted. Warner jumped convulsively when the slug hit him. His gun flew out of his hand. He fell backwards, his hands going out at his sides as if to break his fall. But he was dead before he hit the ground, a trickle of blood oozing from the bullet hole between his eyes.

Carter went forward to check him, nodding when he saw the dead, upturned features; wide eyes staring up sightlessly. Billy never did have the sense to know when he was beaten; so here he was in Arizona, dead as a doornail and far from his old stamping ground. There was no emotion in Carter. These men were known outlaws. He turned to check out the man with the rifle, expecting to see Pete Ward, Billy's long-time sidekick, and nodded when he looked down on the dead man sprawled in the long grass.

It was Pete Ward, with a bullet through his face; dead and bleeding silently. Carter gazed at the corpse's features for some minutes, recalling the days when he had hunted the Benson gang through Texas. They had given him a helluva run, and these last two of the crooked bunch had pushed their luck to the bitter end.

Carter turned away and went back to his grey, his face expressionless but his mind was bursting with harsh memories, for he had faced the Confederates in the Union lines at Bull Run. Shadows were long on the ground as he remounted and continued to Singletree, hoping the shooting did not indicate that his future would continue to be violent.

The lone street that formed the town had two rows of wooden buildings straggling along the trail heading east. Mainly single-storied with false fronts, they consisted of saloons, living quarters and business establishments catering for the inhabitants, and the main street was teeming with vehicles of all kinds – big wagons hauling gold ore to the nearby stamp mills, buckboards taking supplies out to the mining area three miles to the north, and the usual traffic that served the local cattle ranches in the area.

Carter reined in and looked around. His first impressions were not good. He was looking for a peaceful place in which to settle, but there had been another gold strike hereabouts recently and the lust for yellow metal brought a madness that ruined any normal town. Prices shot sky-high, bad people moved in to find what rich pickings they could, and the townsfolk had to endure the inconvenience of the gold seekers, their exuberant, physical excitement showing itself in a near-hysterical eruption of fighting and greed.

The evening was advancing. Lamplight gleamed from windows and doors, shafting through the shadows, and strident noise jarred the senses. The wide street was crammed with vehicles of different sizes. Drovers were shouting hoarsely and using whips on humans as well as horses as the traffic snarled up and animals went down in the dust amid the wreckage.

Music was throbbing wildly in the background, an incessant din – the sound of a fiddle was tangled up with the thump of a saloon piano, with shouting and cursing adding another more menacing tempo to the fiendish-sounding music.

Carter put the grey into the press of wagons, hoping to find the livery barn. As he passed the general store, where a tall, thin man in a soiled white apron was trying to fill the orders of more than one buckboard parked in front of his place of business, it seemed to him that the pace of life had quickened tremendously, affecting even those townsfolk who had no business in the gold strike. It was a wild frenzy that assailed everyone slipping inside the pulsing vortex centred in the street.

The street was a riot of movement, mainly of vehicles trying to drive through spaces too narrow for them. Oil flares stained everything with an odd yellowish colour and gave the whole scene a nightmarish aspect. Carter heard shots sounding above the general hubbub and glimpsed two men facing each other on respective driving seats, using pistols instead of whips to gain the upper hand in their struggle to progress through the melee.

There was a plentiful sprinkling of saloons along the street, and Carter's hopes fell to zero, for this hell-hole was the opposite of what he had hoped to find. Even the sidewalks were jammed with a tide of humans swirling and struggling along, pushing and shouting insults at the wagoneers. Carter looked for an alley that would take him clear of the confusion. He was tired and hungry after his time on the trail, and his grey was near exhaustion, trembling with hunger and thirst. He saw a hitch rail on the left, in front of a big saloon, where there was a vacant spot. Six tired mounts were tethered there, and as he kneed the grey into the remaining space he noticed a woman standing at the end of the rail, then realized that she was bound to it by a short length of rope tight around her wrists.

Carter swung out of his saddle and looked at the woman more closely. She was not tall, not old, and was well-dressed. There was no expression on her attractive face, and when her gaze met Carter's her pale eyes were filled with resignation. The sight of her hands bound to the rail, was so unusual that Carter had to halt and talk to her.

'You look like you're in some kind of trouble, ma'am,' he observed. 'Anything I can do to help?'

'You'll make a load of trouble for yourself if you

11

don't keep moving and forget you saw me,' she replied.

'Who tied you out here?'

'No one you know, and if you know what's good for you then you'll get moving.'

'Who would want to tie you to the rail, and leave you here in this bustle?'

'Are you making it your business?' Her eyes were hard but steady, and Carter's curiosity was aroused by her passive acceptance of the situation.

'Something should be done about it. Haven't any of the locals offered to help you?'

'I appreciate your wish to help me, but I have no desire to be the cause of your death.'

'What's your name?' Carter could not find the will to leave her. 'It's not in me to pass a woman in need of help.' He pulled a long-bladed knife from the sheath fixed to the back of his belt, and lamplight flickered along its length as he slashed through the rope where it rested on the rail.

'Thanks. Now you'd better get out of here before my husband shows up and starts a rumpus. He's in the saloon there, and he keeps a close eye on me despite treating me like a horse.' There seemed to be wild humour in her voice.

'What's your name?' he persisted, and she suppressed a sigh, rubbing her wrists gently as she gazed at him. At that moment a loud voice called from just behind Carter, and he saw her expression change, her fatalistic attitude altering to fear.

12

'I told you my husband kept a close eye on me,' she said quickly. 'You'd better start running, mister.'

Carter took a short step to his left and then pivoted on heel and toe, his defensive movement taking him back out of reach of the clenched fist that was swinging for his head. He caught a glimpse of a huge man, face shadowed by the brim of a ten-gallon Stetson, lunging forward to make contact. His bearded face backed up his swinging right fist. Carter slid away to his left, and the man was momentarily unbalanced, but recovered quickly and lunged closer.

'You was butting into a private matter,' the man accused. 'I saw you cut her free from that rail.'

'Why was she tied to it?' Carter countered. 'I've got a nasty habit of sticking my nose into private matters involving bad treatment of womenfolk, and you deserve to be horse-whipped if you tied her here.'

'I'd kill any man trying to take a whip to me. But if you want to try fists or guns then I'll go along with that.'

'Are you loco? Do you live around here?'

'That's none of your business.'

The woman cried out as the man reached for his gun, and she tried to step in front of Carter who held her off with his left hand and set his gun hand into motion. His gun was clear of leather and gaping at the man before the other could level his weapon. Carter cocked his hammer and jabbed the muzzle

13

into the big body confronting him. The man froze, his pistol spilling out of his hand.

Carter shook his head as he spoke. 'I've just got into town after a long ride, mister, and I'm plumb tuckered out. All I want to do is bed down my horse and then get on the outside of a big steak and a glass of beer. You saw the speed of my draw, so do you still want to fight?'

'The hell I do. I've never seen anything faster than that gun of yours, unless it's a striking sidewinder. I'm Rough Milligan. I own the RF cattle spread ten miles out to the east. Go put away your gear and grab some grub; and keep away from my wife in future.'

Milligan took his wife's arm and dragged her to the boardwalk. Carter holstered his gun and watched them until they vanished into the crowd, and he shook his head at such behaviour. He stepped onto the sidewalk as a buckboard passed him closely at speed and a spinning wheel tagged his elbow. He jumped half a stride to avoid being dragged under the vehicle. His horse swung sideways, tugging at its tether, and Carter shouted at the buckboard driver, who replied with a mouthful of verbal invective.

'I'll take care of your horse, mister,' a voice said at Carter's elbow. 'It ain't safe to leave it on the street these days.'

Carter looked into the face of a young man.

'Are you planning on stealing my horse?'

'I ain't a thief, stranger. My pa runs the livery barn in town, and my job is taking care of horses.'

14

'OK. I'm only joshing.' Carter pulled his saddle bags off the grey and drew his rifle from the saddle boot. 'What's the stable charge for a couple of days?'

'A dollar should cover it. Walt Kelly is my pa's name, and I'm Ryan.' He was a tall, slim eighteen-year-old. He took the dollar that Carter held up and led the grey into the nearest alley.

'Just a minute,' Carter called. 'Is there anywhere in town I can get a decent meal without getting caught up in this crowd?'

'My ma runs a diner, and you couldn't do better than sit at one of her tables. Follow me and I'll show you the way.'

Carter walked behind his grey. There was a lantern on a hook about halfway along the alley, shedding a yellow glow into the dense shadows. Carter kept his right hand close to the butt of his holstered gun, his ears keened for suspicious sounds at his back. They turned out of the alley on to the back lots, where the degree of darkness was diluted by burning lanterns set up at intervals to keep the shadows at bay.

They reached the livery barn, and young Kelly pointed along the street. 'You can't miss the diner from here,' he said. 'And you're in for a treat. My ma is the best cook in town.'

'See you later,' Carter replied, and went on as Kelly led the grey into the stable.

Carter entered the diner and was relieved to see that it was not overcrowded. He sat down at a small table and dropped his saddle-bags by his side. There

15

were ten small tables for diners, and only five of them were occupied. A buxom woman with a kindly face appeared from a back room and confronted him.

'There's a bigger diner along the street,' she said. 'I cater mainly for private eaters.'

'Ryan Kelly took my horse into the stable and pointed me in this direction, ma'am. If you're Mrs Kelly then I've heard that you're the best cook in town.'

Her attitude mellowed, and she smiled. 'Flattery will get you everywhere,' she said.

'I'll have anything that's going.' Carter leaned back in his seat. 'I've travelled a long way, and I need to eat before I try to sleep.'

'Do you plan to stay long in town? I've got a spare room that will be better than any you can rent around here.'

'I'll take you up on that. Now what about the food? I'd sure like to get acquainted with a big beefsteak with all the trimmings.'

'It will be on the table mighty quick.' Mrs Kelly turned and disappeared into the kitchen.

Carter tried to relax while he waited for his meal. He enjoyed the peace of the diner and struggled against tiredness as his body slowly relaxed. He looked up when the street door was thrust open and dropped a hand to his gun butt when a big man entered. The first thing Carter noticed about the newcomer, apart from his height and size, was a law badge with DEPUTY on it, pinned to the front of his

16

red shirt. He looked at the newcomer's face; moon-shaped, ears like a goat and a nose that reminded him of a pig. His greasy corn-coloured hair straggled from under his black Stetson. There was thick dust on the shoulders and breast of his shirt, and when he spoke, his voice rasped like a file working on a piece of hard metal. He wore a pistol low down on his right hip.

'Where's my supper?' he called hoarsely. 'Mrs Kelly, drop everything and get my grub.'

The harsh voice echoed through the diner, and the big man looked around for a seat. He came straight to Carter's table and glared down at him.

'This is my seat when I eat in here,' he said. 'Rattle your hocks, mister, and move.'

'There are unoccupied seats in here,' Carter replied. 'Pick yourself another table for tonight. I'm settled here.'

A frown appeared on the deputy's face and he looked more closely at Carter.

'Are you looking for trouble?' he demanded. His expression had hardened, his eyes narrowed. He gazed at Carter, his manner changing. His eyes widened, filling with shock, and he stepped back from the table. 'Carter?' he growled. 'What are you doing here? They told me you were dead.'

He made a visible effort to recover and then slapped his right hand to the butt of his gun. Carter set his hand into motion; his pistol seemed to leap into his hand and, when he saw the deputy was continuing his draw, he lifted his gun and cocked it. Before the deputy's gun could cover him, Carter fired a shot that slammed into the man's right shoulder.

The blast of the shot sent a string of echoes hammering. The deputy jerked and the gun fell out of his hand. As the weapon bounced on the floor, the deputy went down heavily, taking a couple of chairs with him. His face smacked the floor and he relaxed. A trickle of blood began seeping from his shoulder. Carter got to his feet. The other diners were sitting motionless at their tables, faces showing shock. Carter waited for the gun echoes to fade. His gun was still in his hand, seeming to cover everyone.

'Who is this guy?' he demanded.

'His name is Lou Burton,' someone replied. 'He's one of the local deputies.'

'Did anyone see what happened?' Carter persisted. Silence followed his question, and he nodded. 'So that's the way it is in this town, huh? Everyone's too scared to talk.'

Mrs Kelly emerged from the kitchen, and her arrival broke the prevailing shock.

'No one will answer your questions,' she said. 'In this town it's asking to be shot if you've got a loose lip. There are two other deputies in Singletree, and one of them will turn up pretty soon, for sure.'

'Someone better fetch the doctor,' Carter suggested.

Mrs Kelly shrugged 'He'll be here shortly. He can

18

track down business better than a hound dog.'

The door of the diner was thrust open and a tall man entered. He was wearing a law badge and carried a pistol in his hand. Carter was the only one standing so the man's gun levelled at him.

'Who shot Burton?' The newcomer's gaze flickered around the room.

'He pulled his gun on me,' Carter replied.

'You're under arrest. Drop your weapon and get your hands up.'

'Hold your horses. I shot Burton in self-defence. That ain't against the law.'

'Why did he draw on you?'

'That's the question I want to hear him answer.' Carter was recalling the words that Burton has spoken just before reaching for his gun. He had called out the name Carter, although they were complete strangers, and he suspected the deputy had mistaken him for his brother, Nick, and had pulled his gun immediately. So, Nick was in trouble, and the law department thought he was dead.

Carter tightened his grip on his gun. If Nick was dead, there would be hell to pay. . . .

TWO

'I told you to get rid of your gun,' the deputy rasped. 'You ain't Nick Carter.'

'I'm his twin brother, and you'd better tell me why Burton should think Nick is dead.'

'Nick Carter was with three other men who walked into the local bank last week and withdrew eight thousand dollars at gunpoint. Now you better throw down your gun or try to use it. This is a hell town right now, what with a gold strike booming, and we're going all out to get rid of bad men.'

'I'm not a bad man. I rode with the Texas Rangers for ten years before I turned in my badge, and I'm here to look up my brother. And Nick wouldn't have robbed your bank. We come from a long line of law men.'

'We chased those robbers nigh into Tucson before we got them in our sights, and your brother was one of the two we killed. He wouldn't put down his gun. There's no doubt about that. Now you'd better put away your gun and come along to the sheriff's office.

Sheriff Haskell will want to talk to you.'

At that moment, the diner door was pushed open and a tall, lean man entered carrying a medical bag. He was in shirt sleeves, looked to be in his thirties, and had red hair. His blue eyes were keen, and he looked around quickly but did not speak. He saw Burton lying on the floor; went to his side and dropped to one knee. But he barely checked Burton's wound before he straightened.

'He'll survive,' he said. 'There's no justice in this world.' His gaze lighted on Carter who was still holding his gun. 'Hi, I'm Doc Lyndon. Did you shoot Burton?'

'He says he did, in self-defence,' cut in the deputy.

'He took on both you deputies?' Lyndon sounded amazed. 'You must have been asleep, Milton.'

'Cut the guff, Doc. I ain't in the mood for it.' Milton cocked his pistol, which was pointing at Carter's chest. 'I ain't gonna tell you again to drop your gun, mister. It don't matter to me one way or another which way I take you in. Now get to it.'

Carter opened his fingers and his pistol thudded on the floor. Milton's grin widened. He motioned to the door, and Carter obeyed.

'I've got your meal ready,' Mrs Kelly protested.

'If I ain't back for it within five minutes then perhaps you'll deliver it to the town jail,' Carter said.

Milton crowded Carter as they left the diner, his gun prodding Carter's spine. They walked along the busy boardwalk. Carter moved as if the way was devoid of folk, and when he trod on a man's heels there was a curse and the man swung round, only to fade into the background when he saw Milton with a drawn gun. They walked a block before Carter saw a large building with a big sign on it bearing the legend SHERIFF'S OFFICE & JAIL. Milton grasped Carter's arm and guided him into the law office.

A small man was seated at a desk in a far corner of the office. His feet were up on the desk, crossed at the ankles, and he was reading a book entitled *Western Exploits* by Ned Buntline. He did not look up despite the thud of their boots as they approached the desk, and Milton called roughly.

'I've got a customer for you, Sheriff.'

The sheriff finally looked up, his rugged face showing impatience. He looked at Carter, his blue eyes sharp as the point of a dagger and, as he returned his gaze to the pages of his book, he did a double take. His jaw dropped in shock and he threw his book down on the desk.

'I'm Ben Haskell, the county sheriff. What's your name, stranger?'

'Link Carter, Sheriff.'

'Are you related to a local rancher called Nick Carter?'

'He's my twin brother.'

'And he's dead,' cut in Milton.

'You and Burton haven't produced his body yet, so we can't prove he's legally dead.' Haskell picked up his book, marked the page he had been reading and then put it in a desk drawer. He turned his attention to Milton. 'Did you find out what that shot was about?'

'Yeah, Sheriff.' Milton grinned. 'This guy shot Burton.'

'Did he kill him?'

'No, just winged him. Doc reckons he'll live.'

Haskell's cold eyes fastened on Carter. 'Why did you shoot one of my deputies?'

'He drew on me, and looked like he was gonna kill me, so I shot him in the right shoulder.' Carter fought against impatience as he replied.

'Lock him in a cell, Bud, until tomorrow.' Haskell opened the desk drawer and picked up his book. 'I'll deal with him later. I'm busy right now.'

'There were witnesses,' Carter said.

'They won't testify against a local deputy.' Haskell grinned.

'Can't I come back later?' Carter asked. 'I've been on the trail for weeks, and I'd just paid for a meal at Mrs Kelly's diner when this deputy arrested me.'

'You must be kidding! Lock him in a cell, Bud, and then fetch his food from the diner. You don't seem upset by the news that your brother is dead, Carter.'

'I'll believe that when I see him dead.'

Haskell returned his attention to his book and Milton jabbed the muzzle of his gun against Carter's spine.

'The cells are that way,' Milton directed, pointing to a door in the back wall of the office. 'Don't get any ideas about getting the better of me. I'll shoot you dead if I have to.'

Carter walked the length of the office and opened the door that Milton had indicated. He entered a short passage in a long room which had metal barred doors on either side of a central passage. There were eight cells, and all were occupied. The jail was filled to overflowing. Milton called a halt at one of the doors. He produced a key and unlocked the cell.

'In there,' he rasped.

Carter entered the cell and Milton relocked it and went back to the office. Carter looked around the cell. Three prisoners were in it, lying on single beds. There were two unoccupied beds. An older man – past fifty – sat up and looked at Carter. He was dressed in range clothes.

'Howdy?' he greeted. 'I'm Pete Fargo. You'd better grab one of those empty beds. If they arrest anyone else and you haven't staked a claim, then you'll have to fight for one of them or sleep on the floor.'

The connecting door between the cells and the office was jerked open and the sheriff appeared. He came to the door of Carter's cell.

'Carter,' he said, 'why didn't you say you're a Texas Ranger?'

'Why should I?'

'Come on out of there.' Haskell unlocked the door and Carter left the cell. 'Let's go into the office and talk. Milton has gone to get your meal.'

Carter hadn't had time to think about his brother.

24

He had been shocked by the news that Nick was dead – that Nick had helped rob the local bank, but Haskell had said they hadn't got Nick's body. His head whirled with conjecture, and there was a dim hope in the back of his mind that Nick was still alive.

'So, you're a Texas Ranger, huh?' Haskell mused when they were seated at the desk in the front office. 'Are you in Arizona looking for a fugitive?'

Carter did not correct the sheriff, aware that it could help his situation if he unofficially resumed his former status.

'I can't talk about the job I'm on,' he said.

'I understand.' Haskell nodded vigorously. 'How long have you been a Ranger?'

'More than ten years.'

'That's a lot of experience. I could do with a man like you to help me around here.'

'I can't do that. I'm on a job and the trail has led me here, but I can't get involved in anything without direct orders from my headquarters.'

'Are you by any chance looking into our local law setup?'

'The hell I am! What gave you that idea?'

'You didn't say you're a law man when you were arrested, and you seemed content to sit in that cell as if you didn't have a care in the world. So, what gives?'

'You must have a guilty conscience,' Carter said. 'It's nothing like that.'

'I'm letting you go. Burton ain't badly hurt, and you being a Ranger, he wouldn't have had a legal reason for shooting you, so you had every right to defend yourself against him. You're free to leave.'

'Not so fast. Tell me about my brother. What was the talk about him robbing the bank? And is he dead?'

'I'm sorry to tell you that he was recognized by more than one witness – men who knew him well. A posse chased the thieves almost to Tucson before they turned to fight. Your brother was shot as he leapt off a bluff into a river. He went into the water and was not seen again. The river is fast-flowing, and there are rapids. If the bullet he took didn't kill him then the river would have. That's all I can tell you.'

Carter mused over the information. But there was nothing he could base any hope on. Yet he did not believe Nick would have taken part in a bank raid, and he wondered if his brother had been set up to take the blame. It was likely Nick had come up against the local law – he had done so himself on arrival. They were low-grade law men. He looked up to see Haskell gazing at him.

'What are your plans now?' Haskell demanded. 'Your brother was a cattle rancher, and he was making a success of his business. I expect you'll inherit the place.'

'When was the bank robbery?'

'Last Tuesday; just before closing time. It caught us flat-footed and was all over before we could turn out. We were lucky to get the robbers like we did. It was a helluva chase.'

'Is there a crew out at Nick's place? What stock was he running?'

'I can't tell you much about it. Your brother was an unsociable man. He kept himself to himself, and discouraged visitors to his place. I always felt I was intruding whenever I visited him. There's been a lot of rustling on the range, although your brother never complained of being raided. He ran a real salty crew, and they're still out at the ranch. I think they're hoping that you would turn up there and take over.'

Carter stood up. His gun was lying on a corner of the desk and he picked it up, checking it before thrusting it into his holster.

'I'll be on my way, Sheriff. I've got things to do. See you around.'

'I'm sorry I couldn't be more helpful,' Haskell replied.

Carter picked up his saddle-bags and rifle, which had been dumped beside the desk, and moved to the street door. He paused before opening the door, a thought crossing his mind that he was being released because a gun trap had been set up for him.

'Take a look out at the street in case someone with a gun is waiting for me,' he said.

Haskell gazed at him for several moments before he got to his feet and walked to the door. He opened it and stepped outside, his head screwing around as he checked the street.

Carter stepped in close to him, pushed him aside, and slipped through the doorway to his left, moving swiftly to gain the shadows on the boardwalk. He halted and put his back to the front wall of the law office, his right hand on the butt of his gun.

The sheriff went back into his office and closed the door. Carter ran across the street to the opposite side, dodging the vehicles still lumbering about their business. His thoughts were racing now, and he had some idea of what his next move should be. But first he needed food, and he went back to Mrs Kelly's diner.

Milton, the deputy, was seated at a corner table, eating his way through a thick steak with all the trimmings. A half-consumed glass of beer stood at his elbow. Carter paused beside Milton and said:

'I hope that's not my steak you're eating.'

Milton grimaced, and then grinned. 'I didn't think you'd get around to eating it, so I thought I'd finish it off for you. No sense wasting good food.'

Mrs Kelly came forward, her expression grim. 'I've got your meal on a hot tray,' she said. 'I had a feeling you'd come back. Come into the kitchen. You can eat in there and not be disturbed.'

Carter followed her into the kitchen and sat down at a table the staff used for their meals. Mrs Kelly slid a large filled plate before him and he began to eat hungrily. He felt well satisfied when the steak was in his stomach and he finished the meal with a cup of coffee. Mrs Kelly came to his side.

'Was it to your satisfaction?' she asked.

'Mrs Kelly, I won't have food in any other place

while I'm in town,' he replied. 'I can't recall eating a better meal.' He produced a dollar bill and gave it to her. I'm Link Carter, and my brother, Nick, is a rancher on a local cattle spread. I expect you've heard of him. I heard some bad things about him when I visited the sheriff. Can you tell me what happened to Nick?'

She sat down opposite him and glanced around before leaning forward to speak in a low tone.

'It's not wise for anyone to get loose-lipped around here.' She shook her head. 'The best thing you can do is go into the livery barn and speak to my husband, Walt. Tell him what happened to you when you came in here for a meal, and I'm sure he can tell you what you want to know.'

Carter nodded and got to his feet, picking up his rifle and saddle bags. Mrs Kelly arose and grasped his arm to lead him across the kitchen. She opened the back door and moved into the doorway.

'Go to the left. There are a couple of lanterns to light your way. Follow the path to the barn and you'll find Walt in there.'

'Thank you, Mrs Kelly. I'll see you tomorrow when I get hungry again.'

She smiled and patted his shoulder, and Carter departed. He followed the path to a side door in the livery barn and slipped inside the building. The interior was dimly lit, and he walked through the barn to the front door. A horse kicked a loose board in a stall, and another coughed harshly. The smell of horses was sharp in his nostrils. He saw an office to the right, just inside the big open door, and went to it, frowning as he heard voices coming from within and the sound of a fist striking human flesh. He peered into the office.

A man was cowering against a wall beside a desk in a corner, with a big man standing over him, fist pulled back to deliver a blow. Blood was dribbling from the smaller man's slack mouth.

'Don't hit me again, Swanson,' he pleaded. 'I ain't seen a stranger all evening, let alone talked to one.'

'What's going on here?' Carter demanded, dropping his saddle bags.

The man turned quickly, startled, and lamplight flickered on a deputy badge pinned to his shirt front. He was big, like his two colleagues in the law department, Burton and Milton, and his face was expressing brutality, his lips fixed in a snarl and his dark eyes filled with eagerness. His right hand flashed to the butt of his pistol. Carter swung his rifle and slammed the butt against the deputy's chin. The big man dropped with a cry spilling from his lips. But he surged to his feet and grabbed at his pistol in its holster.

Carter struck again with his rifle, slamming the hard muzzle against the wrist of the deputy's gun hand. The weapon dropped to the floor. Carter kicked it under the desk. He stuck the muzzle of his Winchester under the deputy's chin, forcing his head backwards.

'You better quit while you're still ahead,' he advised. 'What goes on around here? I haven't been in town much more than an hour and already I've clashed with two deputies, and now I find a third one beating the hell out of an old man. What kind of a game have you got going? Is it private or can anyone butt in?'

'You'll be sorry for this,' Swanson said in a blustering tone. 'You're interfering with a law man doing his duty. We got strict laws around here.' He touched his jaw gingerly, his dark eyes filled with a lethal glitter. He was of the same stamp as Burton and Milton, bearded, unkempt, and vicious. Carter was tempted to use the butt of his rifle again but controlled himself.

'You're the livery man, huh?' He looked at the older man, who was slumped against the wall. His thin face was pale, and fear shone in his eyes. 'Why was this big hard-case bullying you?'

'That's the way the law is handled around here. I'm Walt Kelly, stranger. My son brought a grey in a short while ago. Was that your horse?'

'It's mine.' Carter nodded. 'Now tell me what this is all about.'

He held his rifle one-handed, the muzzle still pressing against Swanson's throat. The long gun looked like an over-large pistol in his powerful hands. Walt Kelly moved slowly, sank into the chair at the desk and lowered his face into his cupped hands. Blood dripped slowly between his fingers. Swanson

31

made a convulsive movement – his neck was strained back uncomfortably between his shoulders – and Carter moved fast, removing his muzzle from Swanson's throat and slamming his left fist in a short, powerful punch that hammered his raw-boned knuckles in an explosive impact against Swanson's chin. The deputy slithered down to the floor and stayed there, his eyes shut; his breathing was short and fast.

'That's better,' Carter observed. 'So, what was going on in here when I arrived?'

'Like Swanson said, that's the way the law is handled around here.' Kelly lifted his head from his hands and gazed at Carter. 'You'd better get on your grey and light out of here, stranger. When those other two dogs, Milton and Burton, hear about this they'll be after you, baying like a couple of hounds.'

'I don't think so.' Carter shook his head. 'Burton is at the doc's place right now, having one of my slugs dug out of his right shoulder, so forget about the bullies for a minute and heed what I say. I'm Link Carter. My brother Nick owns a ranch north of town. I heard that Nick is dead, that he took part in a bank raid here recently and was shot by a posse.'

'You're Nick's brother?' Kelly struggled to his feet and stuck out his hand. 'Say, I've heard a lot about you from Nick. He's a good friend of mine and told me about his twin brother who was in the Texas Rangers. I guess he wasn't lying when he said you're one tough guy. But you'll be up to your neck in trouble around here because there are some hard-cases handling the trouble, and they don't care about the law or anyone that tries to stand up against them. Nick ain't dead, and he wasn't with the bank robbers. He wasn't even in town when the bank was robbed. They set him up for that to get rid of him, but he was too smart for them. Now he's lying low for a spell, waiting for you to turn up. He's got a lot of faith in you, Link, and he said that between you, the crooks haven't got a snowball's chance in hell of getting away with their crimes.'

Carter drew a sharp breath of relief at Kelly's words. Nick was alive. He heaved a sigh. Kelly opened his mouth to speak, but his voice was blotted out by the crash of a shot, and before Carter could react, the livery man fell to the floor with blood spurting from a bullet hole in his chest. Carter began to turn, his gun lifting, but a hard voice spoke from behind him.

'Drop the gun or you're dead, Carter. I've got you dead to rights.'

Carter let go of his gun, glancing over his shoulder as he did so. He saw Milton, the deputy, standing in the doorway, a gun in his hand and a curl of gun smoke drifting from its muzzle. . . .

THREE

Swanson staggered to his feet and hit Carter with a right-hand punch. Carter thought his head would come off his shoulders. He dropped instantly, a dark curtain falling before his eyes, blotting out his sight. His hearing remained intact, and he heard Swanson and Milton talking, their voices booming, but his senses were rattled by Swanson's blow and he could make no sense of what was being said. His head was clearing, and he realized dimly that his rifle was still in his right hand.

His sight began to return, blurred at first, and he saw the two deputies again. Milton was bent over Kelly, in the act of ripping open the livery man's shirt.

'He ain't dead,' Milton observed. 'Shall I finish him off?'

'It might be a good idea,' said Swanson. 'We could blame Carter with his murder.'

Carter sat up, bringing his left hand across his

body to grasp the stock of the rifle. His right index finger curled around the curved metal of the trigger.

'I'll start shooting pronto if you two polecats don't drop your guns and put your hands up,' he rasped.

Milton moved fast. He was half-covered by Swanson, and took a chance on shooting Carter, but Carter's rifle cracked, and the slug hit Milton in the head. He went down, arms out flung, and his pistol struck Swanson in the face, knocking him to the floor. Carter jacked another 44.40 cartridge into his breech and levelled the long gun at Swanson.

'The next one will be through your head, Deputy,' he said sharply. 'Drop your gun like I said.'

Swanson remained on his back in a lying position. He threw his gun across the office and raised his hands. Carter got to his feet. His senses swung alarmingly, and he blinked rapidly. Swanson was watching him closely, poised to resist if he got the chance, but Carter was in control of the situation.

'If you so much as blink I'll shoot you,' Carter told Swanson. 'Turn over on your face and stick your hands above your head.'

Swanson obeyed. Carter got to his feet, held his rifle one-handed, and drew his pistol. He stood above Swanson, looking him over.

'If you've got any other weapons on you then now is the time to get rid of them,' he said.

'I've got a knife in a sheath down between my shoulder blades,' Swanson said sullenly. 'You want I should take it out?'

'I'll get it.' Carter pressed the muzzle of his pistol against Swanson's left temple while he reached between the man's shoulder blades. He grasped the handle of a knife and drew it from its sheath; threw it on the desk. He bent over Kelly and saw he'd been hit high in the shoulder and in the chest. 'On your feet, Swanson, we'll call on the doctor on our way to the jail.'

Swanson scrambled to his feet and stood looking at Carter who waved his pistol at the door.

'What are you waiting for? Get moving, and if you try anything you'll never reach the jail alive.'

Swanson hurried out of the office with Carter close behind and met Mrs Kelly.

'What was that shooting I heard?' she demanded. 'Where's Walt?'

'He's in the office,' Carter said. 'He caught a slug in his shoulder. Go in and stay with him and I'll send the doctor here.'

'Who shot Walt?'

'Milton did. He's in the office – dead.'

Mrs Kelly uttered a cry and ran into the office. Carter went on with Swanson leading the way, and the deputy gave no trouble. They paused at the doctor's house, alerted him to the shooting in the livery barn, and then went on to the jail. Ben Haskell was seated at his desk, reading his book, and he looked up with impatience showing on his face when Swanson pushed the street door open. He listened in stony silence while Carter explained what had happened in the barn. When Carter lapsed into silence, Haskell looked at Swanson.

'Did it happen like he said?' he demanded.

'Yeah, I guess it did,' Swanson said sullenly. 'You're not gonna side with him, are you? Milton and me were just doing our duty. This guy was trying to get information from Kelly. You know what a loose-mouth Kelly is. He'll spill his guts at the first opportunity.'

Haskell picked up his cell keys from a corner of his desk. He looked at Carter.

'I'll lock Swanson in a cell until I can get around to him. Is that what you want?'

'Do that and I'll come back in the morning to decide what charges should be made against him.'

'Hey, you ain't gonna take his word against mine, are you?' Swanson demanded.

'He explained what occurred in the barn and you agreed that his account was true, so your word is the same as his, and from what I've heard, I think you and Milton acted far beyond the limits of your duty. You're suspended, Swanson, and you could face criminal charges when the full details are known.'

Carter stood in the office while the sheriff put Swanson behind bars. Haskell was grim-faced when he emerged from the cell block. He threw the cell keys on a corner of his desk, sat down behind it, and looked up at Carter.

'I hope you're not thinking that I condone the actions of my deputies,' he said sharply. 'I'd rather pick a sway-backed horse to wear a deputy's badge than any of the three hard-cases I've been saddled with.'

'Are you telling me they were not acting on your orders?' Carter demanded.

'The hell they were!'

'You didn't pick them as deputies?'

'The hell I did!'

'So, who did?'

'The town council did.'

'Name them. I'll want to know why they put three hard-cases in such a position of trust.'

'Art Forder is the town mayor, and the leader of the town council. He runs the Gay Lady Saloon and some other businesses in the town. Bart Elton runs the general store for Strafford and he's on the council. Then there's George Witting, who owns the gun shop and has an interest in the butcher shop. Frank Thompson owns the hotel, and he's another of the men in power.'

'That'll do. I'll see those men and find out what's going on. Where do you stand in all this, Sheriff? Obviously, you've got no control over your deputies. Do they take orders from you or from someone on the town council?'

'If I don't toe the line with the council then I wouldn't have a job.' Haskell shook his head. 'It's a helluva business, I can tell you.'

'Why do you stay under such conditions?'

'I'm getting a bit long in the tooth now, and jobs

ain't so easy to come by these days.'

Carter picked up his gear. 'I'll see you in the morning. You'll want a statement from me about what happened in the livery barn.'

'I'll go along there now, to see what's doing.' Haskell put his book in the desk drawer and got to his feet, but there was reluctance in his movements, and it showed on his weathered face.

Carter departed. He decided it was time to get a drink and headed for the Gay Lady Saloon. But when he reached the door of the hotel he changed his mind and entered the lobby. He needed a place to rest his head for the night and didn't feel much like sleeping in the livery barn. He crossed to the reception desk, which was unattended, and rang a bell on the counter. A moment later a small man emerged from a back office and came to the desk. He was slightly built, in shirt sleeves, and his yellow hair was brushed straight back off his forehead. His blue eyes were sharp and watchful.

'Good evening, sir, I'm Frank Thompson, the owner of this establishment.'

'I'm Link Carter. I need a room for the night. I'll be gone early in the morning.'

'Yes, sir, I have a room vacant.'

Carter signed the register and Thompson looked at the name he had written.

'I know Nick Carter, who owns the cattle spread north of town. Are you related to him?'

'He's my twin brother. I'll be staying with him for

a spell. Are you on the town council?'

'Yes, I am. As a businessman in town I have a right to help push Singletree in a direction that will satisfy every one of the townsfolk.'

'Did you vote for the appointment of the three deputies, Burton, Milton and Swanson?'

'I did. With another gold rush sending the town wild, we needed some gun-tough men to back the local law, and these three arrived in town at the right moment for us.'

'I killed Milton a short while ago. I've met all three of your deputies, and they were intent on giving me trouble. I didn't like the way they were handling the law.'

'Does the sheriff know about this?' Thompson's face paled and his teeth were clenched.

Carter nodded. 'You haven't done this town any favours, mister, and the sooner you get together with others of the council and undo the mistake you made, the better.'

He took the key that Thompson handed him.

'Up the stairs and turn right. Number fourteen is the second on the left.'

Carter went up to the room and dumped his saddle bags and rifle inside. Locking the door, he dropped his key off at the desk in the lobby and went out to the street. The pandemonium there seemed to have slackened somewhat, and he walked along the board walk until he came to the Gay Lady Saloon. He paused for a moment and glanced around the street before pushing through the batwings and walked into the brightly-lit saloon. He paused on the threshold. The place was crowded. There was no space at the long bar, and all the games of chance were crowded with players. A stage was at the far end of the room, where a pianist was playing accompaniment for a scantily-clad girl who was singing. Standing at the far end of the bar, close to the stage, a big man, immaculately dressed in a blue store suit, frilled white shirt, and a black string tie with a diamond stick-pin in it, was watching the singer intently. He had fair hair, greased and close to his head, and his face had the intensity of a preying lobo wolf.

Carter studied the man, and a thought crystalized in his mind. He knew that face, but could not place it, and bought a beer from a skinny bar tender and stood watching the well-dressed man over the rim of his glass while he enjoyed the beer. By the time the girl finished her song, Carter had recalled where he'd seen the man before. Art Forder had owned a saloon back in Texas and was run out by the Rangers. Carter moistened his lips. Here was a thief from his past. What was Forder doing in Arizona?

Forder must have felt eyes on him for shortly he turned and stared at Carter, who saw realization slowly filter into his expression. Carter turned his attention to the girl singer and it came to him that she was Cassie Canfield, who had been with Forder back in Texas. At that moment Forder appeared in

41

front of him, blocking Carter's view of the girl.

'I know you from somewhere,' Forder said, smiling, 'but I can't remember where. Do you recall me from someplace?'

'You had a saloon in Renton, Texas, as I remember,' Carter replied, 'and you were run out of town for crooked dealing, or something.'

'Yeah, I remember now. You were one of the Texas Rangers that night in Renton.'

Carter grimaced. 'I've quit the law now. I'm here to see my brother who owns a ranch north of town.'

'Which ranch?' Forder's dark gaze never left Carter's face. He was a big man with wide shoulders, and looked every inch a ruthless businessman, a gambler who never backed down from a challenge. His cold, unemotional gaze gave the impression that he was unrelenting.

'My brother is Nick Carter. He owns a cattle ranch north of town.'

'I know Nick. He's had some trouble with a gang operating around here – rustlers, bank robbers and the like. Have you seen the local sheriff yet? There was some bad trouble in town last week and your brother was caught up in it.'

'I've talked to Haskell. I'm heading out to Nick's ranch first thing in the morning.'

'You won't find Nick there. They say he was with the gang that robbed the bank last week. Word is that he was killed by the posse that went out after the robbers.'

'I heard about that, but I don't believe it. I'll check out the business for myself.'

'I hope you'll find it is all a mistake.' Forder's expression did not change. 'When you get through with what you've got to do then come and give me a look. I could do with a man of your calibre. If the bad news about your brother is true then you'll be high and dry around here, and I might be able to put some work your way. See you later, huh?'

Forder smiled, and went back to the end of the bar when Carter did not answer him. Cassie finished her song and joined Forder at the bar. He spoke into her ear and she turned instantly to look at Carter. The next instant she was coming towards him and ignored Forder when he called her back. She had a smile on her face when she reached Carter and held out a slim hand.

'Art told me you were here,' she said. 'I remember you in Texas, Carter, law badge on your chest, the only decent man around. I wasn't even upset when you chased us out of Texas. Are you still in the Rangers?'

'I haven't quit,' he bluffed, and smiled.

'You're not gonna chase us out of here, are you?' She laughed although her blue eyes remained expressionless. Carter was thinking that she hadn't changed from how he recalled her – attractive, shapely, the kind of woman that a man like Forder wanted to have hanging around.

'Is Forder doing anything that makes you say that?'

he countered.

'No. We saw the light after that Texas fiasco. You did us a big favour by moving us on, although we didn't think so at the time. Now we're settled here and doing well, and I'd hate to have to move again.'

'What you get up to now is none of my business.' He shrugged and smiled.

'I'm glad we've got that straightened out.' She leaned close enough that he could smell the perfume she was wearing, and patted his arm. 'Would you come and have a drink with Art and me?'

'Thanks, but not right now. I've been on the trail for weeks, and I got into town only a couple of hours ago. All I'm ready for at the moment is to hit the sack. We'll make it another time, OK?'

She nodded and went back to Art Forder, who took her out of the saloon through a doorway that led to their private rooms.

Carter finished his beer leisurely, his mind busy on the situation, and he did not like what came to mind. He stifled a yawn and decided to call it a day. He was past the point of tiredness. He left the saloon, pausing to place his shoulders against the nearest wall to check his shadowy surroundings before moving on back to the hotel. The street was much quieter now and he sighed with relief. He hoped to find his brother tomorrow, for he discounted what he had been told about Nick's death. Walt Kelly, before he'd been shot, had said Nick was still alive and in hiding, and Link had accepted that as the truth. His tiredness was preparing him for sleep as he entered the hotel, his eyelids drooping. A young woman was standing at the reception desk, and she straightened when she saw him, a tall, willowy girl with an attractive face and shoulder-length brown hair.

'I'm Link Carter,' he said.

'For a moment I thought you were Nick,' she responded, and took his key off the key board and held it out to him, a smile on her lovely face. His fingers touched hers when he took the key and her smile widened. 'I'm Thelma Thompson. My father owns the hotel and he told me of your arrival. I'm a friend of your brother Nick – a very good friend.'

His tiredness vanished. 'So, you're Thelma. Nick wrote me about you. I'm pleased to make your acquaintance, Thelma. I've heard some very disturbing news about Nick since I got here. Can you tell me what's been going on?'

She looked at him with suddenly narrowed eyes, her gaze filled with worry. 'I wish I knew something, but Nick left me here last Sunday evening saying he was going out to the ranch, and I haven't seen him since, or even had a word from him. Then I heard that he was one of the men that robbed the bank, and' – her voice tremored – 'the next thing I heard was that he had been trapped by the posse that went out after the robbers and fell into the river when he was shot.'

Carter shook his head. 'That's the story I heard,

45

but I also heard a different version of what happened, and at the moment I'm inclined to believe that instead of the story going around town.'

Her eyes brightened, and she clutched at his sleeve. 'I wish I could believe that. Anything would be better than the finality of what they're saying.'

He patted her shoulder. 'Don't give up hope. I don't think Nick would ever rob a bank. He's not the type. Something bad is going on in this town and now I'm here I'll get down to cases and get at the truth. There are a couple of things I've already picked up that need checking, so don't despair.'

'I hope to God you are right. Nick has had a lot of trouble lately. Someone is trying to run him off the range.'

'I'll get to the bottom of his troubles. Just give me a little time.' He stifled a yawn. 'I've got to hit the sack now. I'm near out on my feet. I'll keep you informed of my progress.'

'Watch out for the local law. There are three very bad deputies in town.'

'I've already met them. One is dead, and another is in the care of the local doctor. I don't doubt I'll see the third one again when he crawls out of his hole.'

Her expression changed, and she gasped. Carter nodded slowly.

'That's the way it goes in my business,' he said unsmilingly. 'Goodnight, Thelma.'

She nodded silently, and he went to the stairs and ascended swiftly to his room, his thoughts on Nick.

He unlocked the door, reaching for a match to light the lamp, and a gun muzzle inside the room spurted a dazzling discharge almost in his face. He was temporarily blinded by the flash, felt a lightning claw of pain in his left ear, and hurled himself sideways as he reached for his gun.

FOUR

The unknown gun blasted again, very close to Carter, and he felt the stinging strike of lead across his left forearm. His weapon came to hand and, judging the position of his assailant by the muzzle-flash, he lunged forward, gun ready and left hand outthrust to grasp the gunman. His fingers closed on a shoulder, and he struck with his gun barrel as the man tried to get away. The pistol thudded against bone and the man slumped. Carter holstered his gun instantly and used both hands to hold the man. He hauled the dead weight into a sitting position and got behind him, slipping his left arm around his neck. The man was unconscious, and Carter let him go and felt for a match. By its dim light he went to a lamp on a nearby table.

Yellow glare filled the room when he applied the flickering match to the lamp wick, and he turned to survey the man crumpled on the floor. He was not surprised to see a deputy badge glinting on the man's chest, and recognized the heavy features of Swanson, who was supposed to be in jail.

Voices began calling from outside the door, and Carter drew his gun before jerking the door open. Frank Thompson stood in the hall, clasping a shotgun, and he stared at Carter in shock.

'What happened?' Thompson demanded. 'Did someone get killed?'

'Not this time.' Carter went back into the room, grasped Swanson by the scruff of the neck and dragged him out into the passage. 'If the sheriff turns up, send him to me.'

He re-entered the room and locked the door, and then looked around the room, wondering how Swanson got in. When he peered out of the front window he saw a wide balcony running the width of the hotel. The lock on the window was broken. He sat down and checked his gun, reloading the used chamber. Someone knocked at the door, and he got up and opened the door. Sheriff Haskell was outside. Carter looked out into the passage and saw that Swanson was no longer there.

'What happened in here?' Haskell demanded, his tone edged with truculence.

'Swanson was in here waiting for me. How come he got out of jail? You locked him in a cell and he was supposed to remain a prisoner until I came to the jail in the morning. Did you turn him loose?'

'The hell I did! I went for something to eat, and he was gone when I got back. I was out looking for him

49

when I heard the shooting in here.'

'How did he get out of the cell?'

'Had a spare key, I reckon. The lock on the cell was not broken.'

'Where is he now?'

'He's on his way back to his cell. My night jailer was with me, and he's taking him in. Swanson will be there in the morning when you want him.'

'I'll believe that when I see him.' Carter turned to enter his room. 'Goodnight, Sheriff.'

He closed the door, bolted it, and pushed the back of a chair under the door handle. He took off his boots, placed his pistol under his pillow, and stretched out on the bed. Ignoring the slight pain in his left forearm and the sting in his left ear lobe, he closed his eyes and relaxed. In a few minutes he was asleep and did not stir until the sun shone in at the front window next morning and disturbed him.

When he was dressed for the street, freshly shaved and his pistol cleaned, Carter took his saddle-bags and Winchester with him when he went to Mrs Kelly's diner for breakfast. The establishment was busy, and Mrs Kelly came to his side when she saw him, wiping her hands on a cloth.

'How's Mr Kelly?' he asked.

'The doc treated him last night. He reckoned Walt would be OK in a couple of weeks, barring complications. Thank you for taking Walt's part against those hoodlums. Did Walt know anything that would help you?'

'He told me what I hoped to hear, but I've got to set to work to make sense out of what I learned.'

'You didn't come back here to sleep.' Mrs Kelly shook her head. 'You went to the hotel and got some more trouble.'

'I live on trouble. I wouldn't know what to do without it.'

'I hope things work out for you. You can eat here for nothing anytime while you're still around. But I don't hold out much hope for you, up against the whole crooked shebang on your lonesome. You've already learned that the local law is no good but wait until you come up against Clem Strafford and his C Bar S crew. He owns just about everything on the range south of town, and he's aiming to gobble up everything else within reach. I expect your brother's trouble has its roots at C Bar S.'

'Thanks for the information. I'll check it out when I can get round to it.'

After breakfast he went along to the law office and was faintly surprised to find the sheriff at his desk, with Swanson in leg irons, seated opposite.

'Morning,' Haskell greeted him.

Carter gave him a disapproving look. 'What gives?' he demanded.

Haskell smiled. 'Swanson and me are accustomed to playing cards together, and I don't see why I should forego that pleasure just because he's been jailed. I put leg irons on him so he can't run away.' He got to his feet. 'Come on, Buster, back to your cell now.'

51

'Leave him be now he's out here,' Carter said. He subjected Swanson to a long, hard look. 'Why did you get into my hotel room last night, Swanson? And how did you know I'd got a room there?'

'You killed Milton. He was my friend, so I reckoned to kill you.'

'You've got a clear-cut case of attempted murder against him,' Haskell said eagerly. 'I can hold him on that.'

'Do it,' Carter turned away. He could see which way the wind was blowing and knew further talk would be a waste of time. 'I've got other things to do today. I'll be back later to handle Swanson.'

'If you're gonna try and find out what happened to your brother then you'd do well to take Swanson along. He was leading the posse when they caught up with the bank robbers.'

Carter clenched his teeth. 'So, Nick was set-up, huh?' he demanded.

'There's no proof of that,' Haskell replied.

'Don't let Swanson out of his cell before I get back,' Carter warned. 'The next time it happens I'll do something about you, Sheriff.'

Carter went along to the livery barn for his grey and found Ryan Kelly in his father's office. The youngster got to his feet when Carter walked in, and came around the desk to grasp his hand.

'Thank you for saving my father's life last night. I wish I'd been here. I would have killed that bullying deputy. The whole law department, sheriff included, should be kicked out. They're a disgrace, and the honest folk in town deserve better.'

'I agree with you.' Carter permitted a smile to flicker across his lips. 'I've made some changes around here already, and it won't stop there. But what I need right now is some information about what happened before my arrival. Your pa told me last evening that my brother was not involved in the bank robbery and didn't get shot by Swanson or fall to his death in the river. If that is the case, then Nick is still alive somewhere and I've got to locate him fast.'

'Nick is a friend of my family. I know he didn't take part in the bank robbery, but I don't know where he is.'

'OK, then tell me how to get out to the N Bar C ranch. There must be some of Nick's crew out there.'

'And what a crew! Two of them are working under cover for Strafford, and the others are more like gunmen than cowpokes.'

'Just tell me how to get out there,' Carter said.

'Turn right out of here, and when you leave town, follow the trail to the big fork, and take the right-hand one. The first cattle spread you come to is N Bar C.'

'Thanks. Where's my grey?'

'It's ready-saddled in the last stall on the left. I guessed you'd be riding out early, and I figured it would be better if you left by the back door.'

Carter took his leave and was relieved as he rode

away from the livery barn. He left town and cantered until he reached the fork in the trail. An open trail beckoned him, and he pushed the grey into a mile-eating lope. He gazed around, hard-eyed and ready for trouble, and his thoughts were centred on what had occurred since he'd entered the town the previous evening. But Nick was the most important factor in the unfolding situation, and Carter rode steadily until he came to a bob-wire fence with a gate in it and a large sign over it. N BAR C was burned into a flat piece of timber, and underneath in smaller letters was his brother's name.

Carter studied the board for several moments. The range sloped upwards from the gate to the nearest skyline. A smudge of smoke showed above the rise. Carter leaned over in his saddle and unfastened the gate, passed through, and paused to close the gate. As he straightened, a gun crashed and he heard a bullet crackle in his left ear. Echoes hammered away into the distance with decreasing volume. Carter sprang out of his saddle, stood with his grey between him and the direction from which the shot had come, and remained motionless, his eyes searching the area for signs of gun smoke.

Two riders suddenly emerged from a depression some fifty yards from the gate. They were armed with rifles and came forward at a canter, weapons pointed at the gate. Carter watched, noting their appearance. Both were range dressed, narrow Texas leg chaps, leather vests and neckerchiefs, and broad-brimmed

Stetsons. In addition to their rifles, both were armed with pistols on their hips. They came to within a few yards of where Carter waited and reined in. One was tall and lean, with hard, thin features and cold blue eyes; the other was shorter, and tubby – with a fixed grin on his thin lips. But he had the same cold stare in his eyes as his partner. Carter remained behind his horse, his right hand down at his side, the butt of his holstered Colt just touching the inside of his wrist.

'Where do you think you're going, Buster?' demanded the lean man.

'I want to see Nick Carter.'

'What's your business with him?' the other man asked.

'I'll tell Nick when I see him. How come you're riding herd on the gate? Have you got trouble around here?'

'Nick ain't here, and it looks like he won't be back, ever,' the thin man said. 'I'm Nat Dupree. I'm running this place while Nick is away. So, what do you want?'

'I'm Nick's brother, Link. I've come from Texas to see him.'

Neither man showed any change of countenance at Carter's words, but Dupree jacked a cartridge into the chamber of his Winchester.

'Like I said, Nick ain't here, so you'd better get out while the going is good,' Dupree said harshly.

'Didn't you hear what I said? Nick is my brother. He must have talked to his crew about me.'

'I ain't his crew. I ride for Strafford of C Bar S. You're on private property, Mister, so get off this range while you can.'

Carter shook his head. 'I've heard about Strafford. He's a land shark. Has he put you in here? And why have Nick's loyal crew let you take over?'

'I told you. Nick left me in charge while he was away.' Dupree grinned. 'There's no one here can outdraw me so what I say goes. What are you gonna do about it?'

Carter grasped the butt of his pistol and thumbed back the hammer. Dupree heard the clicks and started the muzzle of his rifle upward.

'Hold it,' Carter said sharply. 'If you point your gun at me I'll start shooting.'

'Turn her loose!' Dupree called, his rifle beginning to level.

Carter palmed his gun and swung it over the grey's back. He triggered a shot even as Dupree worked the action of his rifle. Carter's gun blasted, and Dupree could not continue his action. He dropped his rifle and swayed in the saddle as his mount jerked away. The animal reared and Dupree lost his balance and fell backwards to the ground, his right foot trapped in his stirrup. The horse ran, dragging Dupree. Carter turned his gun on the other man, who sat frozen in his saddle, his face showing shock.

'What are you gonna do?' Carter demanded. 'Work your gun or throw it away.'

The man discarded his rifle as if it had suddenly

become too hot to hold. He controlled his horse with his knees and raised his hands shoulder high. He was young and did not have the look of a hard-case about him. His fleshy face was pale, and his eyes were clear of intention.

'Get down and shuck your gun belt,' Carter rapped. 'What are you called? You work for Strafford as well, huh?'

'No. I don't work for Strafford. I'm Jake Mortimer. I'm your brother's man, as Dupree was supposed to be. This is the first time I heard Dupree is working for Strafford.'

Mortimer vacated his saddle and unbuckled his gun belt. He dropped it in the grass.

Carter was watching Dupree's horse which had stopped thirty yards away and was now grazing. Dupree was still trapped by the foot caught in the stirrup.

'So where is my brother Nick?' Carter demanded.

'I don't know. He ain't been around for almost a week. He rode out the day before the bank in town was robbed. I was shocked when I heard he was one of the bank robbers. A posse gave chase, and there was shooting when they caught up with the robbers. It was said that Nick was one of them, and he fell into the river when he was shot and wasn't seen again.'

'I've heard that story and I don't believe it. How many are there in the crew here?'

'Three. Denny Dolan ain't loyal to the brand; he rode in with Dupree. They showed up here a couple of weeks ago, hunting a job. Nick took them on because they were good with their guns. But I think Nick knew who they really were, that they were working for Strafford. Not much escapes Nick's eyes.'

'Nick knows how many beans make five,' Carter agreed. 'Where's the rest of the crew?'

'They're in the ranch house, just over that rise.' Mortimer pointed. 'I reckon they heard the shots so now they might be on their way here, loaded for bear. We've been watching for trouble because Nick ain't around.'

'Mount up and let's go face them.' Carter swung into his saddle. 'Pick up your hardware and strap it on.'

Mortimer complied and swung into leather. He rode in beside Carter and they ascended the rise. Before they were halfway to the top, three figures appeared on the skyline and reined in. Carter saw them pull their rifles, but they made no attempt to use them.

'They can see it's me with you,' Mortimer said. 'That tall one on the right is Denny Dolan. He's real fast with a gun.'

They reached the riders and reined in. The newcomers held their rifles ready but did not point them at Carter.

'What was that shooting we heard?' Dolan asked.

'Dupree stuck his neck out and lost,' Mortimer said.

'And who's your friend?' Dolan persisted.

'Do you have to ask?' Mortimer grinned. 'Just look at him and tell me who you think he looks like.'

'He's got the look of Nick about him,' another said. 'Is that who you are, mister – Nick's brother?'

'I'm Link Carter, and Nick is my brother. Who are you three?'

'That one on the left is Denny Dolan,' Mortimer said. 'The one in the middle is Charlie Morrow; the other is Pete Attew.'

'I heard Dolan rides for Strafford? Is that true, Dolan?'

Dolan was like a beanpole. His face was long and thin, his chin pointed, and his dark eyes were bright like a bird's. Carter had dropped his hand to his holstered gun as he rode up, and was ready for action. He watched the lowered muzzle of Dolan's rifle. There was a controlled eagerness in Dolan's body. He was like a spring under pressure, ready to unleash its power.

'Why don't you drop the rifle so we can talk?' Carter suggested. 'I reckon you know a lot about what's going on around here, and I'd sure like to learn about it.'

Dolan looked at Carter for several tense moments. When he spoke, his words came out in a rush.

'Where's Dupree?' he demanded.

'He's dead,' Carter told him. 'He made his play and came second.'

Dolan lifted his rifle as if it was heavy like a cannon. Before he could aim it at Carter he saw

Carter's pistol appear in his hand and explode in fire and smoke. The bullet hit him in the chest and blasted through his heart. He fell from his saddle, dead before he hit the ground. Echoes faded, and silence returned. The cowpokes sat motionless, shocked, staring down at Dolan's body. Carter broke the silence.

'I came here to visit with Nick,' he said, 'but, considering the situation, I'll take over here and run the place until I know what's happened to my brother. If any of you don't like that idea, then you can quit. So, think about it and let me know what you decide. In the meantime, can anyone throw some light on what's been going on? Who saw Nick in the bank with the robbers? I know my brother wouldn't do anything illegal to save his life, so I reckon someone was telling lies. And what's the trouble with Strafford? Why has he sent gun men in here? What's he after?'

'We heard from Sheriff Haskell that the banker, Henry Maddock, identified Nick as one of the robbers.' Mortimer elected himself to be the spokesman. 'What Strafford is after is anyone's guess, although it's plain and simple to me. He wants this spread. He needs more acres to run his herds on.'

'You can ask Strafford himself what's on his mind,' Charlie Morrow said quickly. 'He's coming this way now with three men, and he looks loaded for bear.'

Carter heard the thudding of approaching hoofs and looked towards the gate. He saw a big man on a white stallion, leading three other riders, and for a moment it looked as if the rancher was going to try and jump the obstacle. But he pulled his horse to a skidding halt and one of his men hurried forward to open the gate. Strafford was big, and then some, running to fat. He sat his saddle as if he was in an armchair and drove his spirited stallion with brute strength. The quartet came on, leaving the gate swinging, and headed straight for the riders clustered around Carter, who could hear Strafford's strident voice cursing his horse and his men.

Carter kneed his horse some yards forward of Nick's crew to be the first man the newcomers would reach.

'Just sit still,' he said over his shoulder. 'I'll handle this.'

Strafford forced his mount up the rise and did not rein in until the last possible moment. His stallion's head almost struck Carter's horse and, when it was within reach, it tried to bite the grey. Carter held his ground and gazed at Strafford, who looked even larger and more formidable close up. Strafford's riders reined in a few yards back and spread out in a half circle, hands close to their guns. They looked a hard-bitten bunch.

'Who in hell are you?' demanded Strafford, glaring at Carter. His gaze swept around, taking in the tense faces of the cowpokes backing Carter, and then he saw Dupree's horse farther back, and Dupree with his foot still hung up in a stirrup. 'Say,

61

that's Dupree's horse over there. Is that Dupree down?'

'Sure is,' Carter replied smoothly. 'He tried to shoot me, so I had to kill him. If you look a bit harder down the slope, you'll see Dolan is also dead – shot for the same reason.'

Strafford cursed, and his stallion cavorted, almost unseating him. He curbed the animal with brute strength, sawing powerfully on the reins, sending it into a series of jumps and leaps, crawfishing and squealing in rage. When Strafford got the animal under control he kept it on a tight rein, but it snorted and fought him ceaselessly.

'I asked who in hell you are,' Strafford snarled. His pale eyes were filled with aggression, his mouth twisted by passion. 'Larkin, have you got your eyes on this man? He's a trouble-maker, and you've got my permission to shoot him if he gives us any trouble.'

'I'm watching him, boss,' a small, slightly-built man said.

Carter had been watching the men with Strafford and figured Larkin was the most dangerous of the newcomers. He was holding his reins in his left hand and his right hand was resting lightly on his right thigh, close to his holstered pistol.

'I'm Link Carter. My brother is Nick Carter, who owns this spread, and I'm gonna run the place until I find out what's happened to my brother. If there's any shooting to do around here then I'll do it, Strafford, so hold off because you'll get my first slug if you don't keep your men under more control than you've got over your horse. What do you want here, anyway? You left the gate open when you came in, so if you visit again, then stay the other side of the gate until you get invited in.'

Strafford cursed and dropped a hand to his gun butt. Carter caught the start of the movement and set his hand in motion. His gun cleared leather and the muzzle pointed at Strafford's chest, the three clicks sounding menacingly loud as the weapon was cocked. Carter saw Larkin move his hand in the direction of his gun and called out sharply.

'Strafford gets my first slug dead centre if anyone here clears leather. You're looking death in the face, Strafford, so warn your men off if you want to survive.'

Carter was grinning as he spoke. His challenge had been issued loud and clear, and he waited patiently for a reply. . . .

FIVE

Strafford froze in his saddle as he heard the grim warning, and looked into the black hole of Carter's muzzle as awareness of his bad situation burst like a ray of sunlight in his brain. His heart seemed to miss a beat and a fine sheen of perspiration broke out on his wide forehead. He looked at Carter's face, saw determination there, and deadly intention in his eyes.

'No shooting,' Strafford said instantly. 'I'm here to check for rustled stock. There was a raid on my spread last night – five hundred head gone – and we trailed them in this direction.'

Carter lowered his gun but kept it in his hand, the muzzle loosely covering Strafford.

'If you're following tracks and they pass through here then go ahead and take a look around. But don't come back this way. I don't want to see you twice in the same day.'

Strafford swung his horse and rode away, motioning for his men to follow him. When they were out of earshot, Mortimer laughed harshly.

'You threw a bad scare into Strafford, and even his pet gun hand was cowed. They ain't seen the like of your gun play around here before.'

'I reckon I'll see that bunch again before this trouble is over,' Carter mused. His eyes narrowed as he watched Strafford and his three riders moving across Carter grass at a fast clip. 'I'll just mosey along behind Strafford and find out what he's up to. You men stick close to the ranch house and keep an eye on things. I'll be back later.'

'I reckon you should have one of us along with you,' said Jake Mortimer, glancing at his two colleagues. 'I'll tag along, if you don't mind.'

'You can tail me,' Carter decided. 'I'll follow Strafford and you keep me in your sight. Then if I ride into trouble you'll be in the clear, although I don't know what you can do.'

'I'll cover your back,' Mortimer said.

Carter turned his horse and went after Strafford, who was crossing the ranch yard, followed by his three men. When they had passed around the corner of the house and out of sight, Carter followed, and when he reached the corner of the house he saw Strafford making for the nearest skyline – and there were only two riders with him. It didn't take Carter long to spot that the missing rider was Larkin. He glanced around, and saw Larkin heading off to the right. Carter sighed and settled down to his work.

He looked for fresh cattle tracks coming onto Carter grass and moving through but saw none. He kept an eye on his back, feeling uneasy because Larkin had turned off, but there was now no sign of the gunman. When he looked for Mortimer he saw the cowpoke behind and staying well back.

Strafford was riding as if he expected to be followed. The big rancher did not look left or right and rode for two hours before veering to his left and continuing at a faster pace. Carter reined in and sat watching, trying to figure what was in the big rancher's mind. Mortimer came up alongside him.

'What going on, boss?' he demanded.

'I think Strafford knows I'm behind him and he's just wasting my time. Did you see anything of Larkin? He left Strafford when they went around the corner of the house.'

'I didn't see him. Where do you reckon he's gone? He'll be up to something, I'll bet.'

'Let's go back to the ranch house.' Carter changed direction and retraced his trail. He pushed into a run with Mortimer following closely and did not slacken the pace until he saw the ranch house in the distance. When he saw smoke curling up from the building he spurred his horse and went on at a gallop. Mortimer had to push his mount hard to stay abreast.

As they drew nearer, Carter could see that the house was blazing furiously. The roof fell in even as he made out some of the details, and he knew the fire was out of control. He spotted two figures lying on the ground in the yard and drew up beside them. Morrow and Attew were dead, and their guns were on the ground.

'Check them out,' Carter said. 'I'll look for Larkin. Wait here until I get back.'

He went on around the house and rode for the spot where he had last seen Larkin. A single set of horse tracks were plain in the lush grass. He followed them intently, found a spot where the horse had halted and saw the prints of boots going on to the rear of the house. He could get no closer to the building because of the fire but followed boot tracks and entered the barn. He saw a tank in a corner where kerosene was stored, and worked his way back, still following tracks to the rear of the house.

An empty kerosene can was lying close to the back door. Larkin's boot prints showed where he had entered the house and come out again. The tracks led back to where Larkin's horse had waited, and Carter reached a spot where grass had been trampled down. He saw the gleam of metal in the grass and picked up two used 44.40 rifle cartridges, bright in the sunlight. He read the grim signs of what had occurred. Larkin had stood out here until Morrow and Attew fled from the fire, and then shot down

67

both men in cold blood.

Mortimer came across the yard, his face showing uneasiness. 'A couple of riders are coming in from the east,' he reported.

Carter checked the tracks of Larkin's horse before leading the way into the yard and looked for details. He noted the rear right shoe bore a vee-shaped nick where it had struck a stone and a sliver of metal had been chipped out, and the left fore-shoe had a bar across its centre to strengthen it. He stored the information in his mind and was fixing the details in his memory while he and Mortimer were standing by the bodies of Morrow and Attew. Two riders appeared from around the back of the barn and rode towards them.

'It's Rough Milligan and his wife Susan,' Mortimer said in a harsh whisper. 'He's not to be trusted. Milligan acts as if he feeds on loco weed half his time, and he's got a nasty habit of tying his wife to a hitch rail in town when he's afraid she might stray.'

'I've met him. I wonder what he wants.'

'He's got a shoestring ranch just north of us, and he's always dropping in when he wants to borrow something,' Mortimer added.

They watched the big man's approach. Milligan's face was expressionless as he drew near. He motioned his wife to halt and rest. Carter studied her. She still had an expression of resignation on her face, and Carter wondered if Milligan was in the habit of beating her, although she bore no signs of violence. She gazed at Carter as if she hadn't seen him before, and he turned his attention to Milligan.

'Howdy?' Milligan greeted in an over-loud voice. He peered at Carter and his expression changed. 'Say, don't I know you from some place? Were you in town last night?'

Mrs Milligan suddenly became animated, and she shook her head at Carter.

'No,' Carter said. 'I wasn't in town last night.'

'You look mighty like Nick Carter.'

'That's because I'm his twin brother. I was here last night. Did you know Nick has gone missing?'

'I've just seen that his ranch house has burned down. I saw the smoke from way back. He told me the last time I saw him that he was having trouble with rustlers. So, what happened? Is there anything I can do to help? Nick has been kind to me – helped me a lot in the past.'

'We can manage,' Carter said, 'but thanks for your offer.'

'Do you want me to tell the sheriff about the fire? I'm heading into town.'

'I'll tell him myself. I'll be riding in later.'

Milligan shook his reins. 'I'll be on my way then.' He motioned to his wife and she touched her mount with her heels to follow her husband, who rode on ahead. As she passed Carter she leaned towards him, her gaze upon her husband, and spoke in an undertone.

'Find out where our place is and drop by some-time very soon, Mr Carter.'

He gazed after her, wanting to ask questions, but she did not look round.

'It would be more than your life is worth to go and see her,' Mortimer said, shaking his head. 'Milligan would shoot you for certain if you showed up at his place.'

'Does Mrs Milligan make a habit of asking folks to drop by and see her?'

'I've never seen her talk to anyone. She's as strange as Milligan, but I guess that's to be expected, her being married to him.'

Carter watched Milligan and his wife ride out of sight, and then turned his attention to his situation.

'I'm gonna follow Larkin's tracks. I want to talk to him about why he burned down the ranch house.'

'It'll have to be gun talk,' Mortimer said. 'Larkin won't let you within a mile now. He's probably lit out for good. He's well in with those deputies in town.'

'That's good news.' Carter picked up his reins and swung into his saddle. 'Your job is to keep an eye on this place,' he told Mortimer, looking down at him. 'I'll be back as soon as I've seen Larkin. Don't get yourself into any trouble. Just make a note of anyone who calls.'

'I'll be here waiting,' Mortimer promised.

Carter touched spurs to his grey and departed, his mind alive with thought. When he reached the outskirts of Singletree he straightened in his saddle and checked his pistol. Now he wanted to see Larkin.

Main Street was still clogged with wagons, and Carter avoided it and headed for the livery barn. He found Ryan Kelly in the loft, forking down straw for bedding in the stalls. The youngster came down the ladder immediately.

'There were a couple of men in here earlier, talking about you,' he said. 'One was trying to get the other to ride with him to help kill you – they'd split five hundred dollars for the job.'

'Who were they?'

'I knew one of them – Todd Harmer. He hangs out in the big saloon owned by Art Forder.'

'You've said enough. I know Forder from Texas. I'll talk to him later. Do you know a gunhand named Larkin who rides for Strafford?'

'Yeah, I know him. He's a bad man to cross. Are you going after him?'

'Has he come in here this morning?'

'He left his roan in the stall over there. I watched him when he left. He went into Forder's saloon.'

'Thanks. I might be able to kill two birds with one stone.'

'Are you going to walk into the saloon and kill Larkin? What's he done?'

'I'll kill him if I don't like his answers to my questions. Take care of my grey, Ryan. I want to check the shoes of Larkin's horse before I call him out.'

'This way,' Kelly said eagerly, and hurried to a stall.

71

'Which shoe do you want to check?'

'The back right.'

Kelly patted the roan and lifted its right back foot. Carter saw a vee in the shoe and nodded. 'Now look at the left fore-shoe. Tell me if it's got a bar to strengthen it.'

'It's got a bar, like you said,' Ryan observed.

Carter looked for himself and nodded. 'That's good enough. If Larkin comes back here, then see which way he rides when he leaves.'

Kelly nodded vigorously. Carter departed, and Kelly led Carter's mount into the stable, but hurried out to the street and followed Carter at a distance, his heart thumping. Carter entered the saloon and paused on the threshold to look around. He saw Forder at the bar down at the far end, and spotted Larkin about halfway along the bar, talking to a tall cowpoke.

The time was about an hour to high noon. A dozen men were in the saloon. It was siesta-time. The bar tender was moving lethargically. Forder looked Carter's way and lifted a hand in greeting. Carter ignored him and walked along the bar until he reached Larkin, who looked up as Carter halted. The gunman's hard features became set and his teeth clicked together.

'You want something, mister?' he demanded.

'Tell me why you burnt the ranch house on N Bar C earlier and murdered two of the crew; Charlie Morrow and Pete Attew.'

'Me? Are you crazy?' Larkin tried to back away from the bar, but Carter reached out and grasped his right arm. Larkin tried to pull free but was unable to do so. His holstered gun was on his right hip and Carter was preventing him from reaching it. Larkin lifted his left hand and snatched at the holstered gun on the cowpoke's hip beside him. Carter clenched his left hand and struck Larkin on the chin.

Larkin stopped moving and fell to the floor like a tree that had been struck by lightning. The cowpoke backed off, raising his hands and shaking his head.

'I ain't involved in what's going on,' he said quickly.

'Get out of here,' Carter rapped, and the cowpoke turned and hurried to the batwings.

Larkin was unconscious, breathing heavily. Carter heard footsteps from further along the bar and glanced up to see Forder coming towards him.

'Stay back, Forder,' he called, and the footsteps halted.

Carter bent over Larkin, took his gun, and stuck it in his belt. The batwings creaked, and he looked up to see Sheriff Haskell peering into the saloon.

'You're just in time, Sheriff,' Carter said. 'Arrest this man.'

'What's the charge?' Haskell came across to the bar.

'He burned the N Bar C ranch house this morning and killed Morrow and Attew.'

'You got proof?'

'There's enough to hold him on.'

'Larkin is one of Strafford's top gun hands. It ain't easy to bring any of that crew to justice.' An edge of doubt lined the sheriff's voice. 'You got to be sure of your facts before you stick your neck out.'

Carter was watching Larkin's face, and saw the man was recovering his senses. Larkin sat up and stared into the barrel of Carter's pistol.

'On your feet, Larkin. You're under arrest.'

'You got the wrong man,' Larkin said through his teeth, 'and you'll be sorry you tangled with me.'

Carter bent at the waist, took hold of Larkin's collar, and pulled him to his feet. Larkin staggered, and then made a grab for Carter's gun. He got a hand to the barrel before Carter hit him with his left fist. Larkin went down again. The sheriff jumped forward, drawing his pistol, and stuck the muzzle against Larkin's left temple. Larkin tried to get up, and then slumped back into the sawdust.

'Can you put him behind bars without my help?' Carter asked the sheriff.

'How do you think I managed before you arrived?' Haskell demanded.

'OK, take him away. I've got a couple of things to do before I leave here.'

Haskell removed Larkin from the saloon at gunpoint. Carter settled his pistol in its holster and walked the length of the bar to where Art Forder was standing. The big saloon man forced a smile when he was confronted.

'I was coming to help you when you were arresting Larkin,' he said.

'Did I look as if I needed help?' Carter demanded.

Forder shook his head. He remained silent, and Carter watched him for a moment or so, noting his expression and general manner. Forder had something on his mind and Carter wondered what it could be. Forder's eyes flickered. He could not stand the suspense.

'Is there something I can do for you?' he asked.

'Tell me about Todd Harmon?'

'Harmon? What's he been up to?'

'It came to my notice this morning that he was talking to another man, trying to induce his friend to help him kill me for a share of five hundred dollars.'

Forder looked guilty, Carter thought. His face had changed colour and his hands went temporarily out of control. He started to speak, thought better of it, and closed his mouth. When he met Carter's eyes he forced a grin.

'I expect that has happened to you many times in the past, huh? How do you cope with this kind of situation?'

'I talk to men I think might want me removed and can pay for the job, and I go to work on the most likely. In view of your past I think you might want me out of the way. Harmon works for you, so it isn't hard to conclude that you know something about Harmon's present activity.'

'I told you I was finished with that kind of business.

I turned over a new leaf when you ran me out of Texas. Sure, I didn't like it at the time, but that's in the past. I don't know anything about anyone wanting you dead, Carter, and I hope you'll believe me.'

'Harmon does work for you, huh?'

'Sure, in a casual way. He does small jobs, running errands and the like. I don't think he can hold down a regular full-time job.'

'Where is he now? If someone is asking for help to kill me then I need to talk to him.'

'He's got the day off. As I recall, said he was going fishing. There's a lake a couple of miles out of town to the east that's popular with the local men.'

'Fishing sounds like an easier proposition than trying to kill me,' Carter observed. 'I hope for his sake he's made the right choice, for his health.'

Carter left the saloon and paused outside to look around the main street. The clutter of wagons of all types and sizes was as bad as ever, and he knew what steps he would take to remedy the crush and relieve the town's anguish. He would make the ore wagons bypass the town.

He walked to the bank and entered. The place was deserted except for a sleepy-looking teller behind the counter. A door in the back wall stood half-open, revealing an office, and there was an overweight man inside seated at a desk. He wore a light-blue town suit and sat slumped in his seat, his chin resting in his cupped right hand, which he was using as a prop for his head.

Carter walked to the door and knocked on it. The man stirred and looked up, then levered his fat body out of the chair and came to the door, his fleshy face filled with question.

'I'm Link Carter, brother of Nick Carter, who owns the N Bar C ranch.'

'I'm Henry Maddock, the banker. Is there something I can do for you?' He was tall and big framed, hard-eyed, and there were shadows of worry in his gaze.

'I heard about the bank raid last week, and you stated my brother was one of the robbers.'

'My statement to the law is on public record. I saw the robbery and gave the truth of what I saw. No doubt you don't like the thought of your brother being criminally involved, but that's the way it stands, and if you've got anything to say about it then you'd better do your talking to the sheriff.'

'I merely wanted to ask if you might have been wrong about Nick,' Carter said patiently. 'Witnessing the robbery, you would have been excited, scared, and maybe saw someone in the gang that merely looked like my brother.'

'I'm sorry. I made a statement about what I saw and there was no mistake about your brother. It was him, right enough, and I wasn't surprised to see him with the robbers. He was in bad trouble money-wise – I showed him the door of my office the previous week because there was nothing I could do to help him. So I guess I wasn't surprised to see him in here with a gun in his hand.'

'You seem pretty much rooted against Nick. Did you recognize any of the other robbers?'

Maddock shook his head. 'It was enough that I recognized your brother. Now if you'll excuse me, I'm busy at the moment. Go and talk to the sheriff if there's anything else on your mind.'

Carter stood his ground as the banker tried to get him moving towards the door, and for a moment they stood chest to chest, looking into each other's eyes. Then Carter put the palm of his right hand on Maddock's chest and pushed him back with such force that the heavier man almost lost his balance. He fell sideways and leaned against the wall at his side, surprised by Carter's action, and then straightened quickly and backed off.

'Where do you come off, trying to push me around?' Carter demanded brusquely. 'I dropped by to talk to you, and you're ready to come at me head to head, as if I were one of your robbers. Take it easy, Maddock. I expect there will be a lot of questions asked about that bank robbery, and you better start thinking about what you're going to tell folks.'

'I'm sorry,' Maddock said, shaking his head. 'It was such a gruelling experience, I haven't recovered from it. Come and see me in a few days and we'll talk again.'

Carter nodded and left the bank. He stood outside

on the sidewalk to consider Maddock's initial attitude and decided that he did not like it at all. He felt
a quickening of his senses, like a blood hound
picking up the scent of a trail he had been following
but lost, and he went on to the law office, his mind
filled with a whole new set of questions that needed
answers. . .

SIX

Entering the jail, Carter found Sheriff Haskell full of menace, interrogating Larkin, a gun in his hand. Larkin was shaking his head. Both men froze when Carter walked in on them. Larkin snarled like a she-wolf and Haskell, who had been talking nineteen to the dozen before Carter arrived, shut his mouth and clenched his teeth.

'There's no need to question him,' Carter said. 'I'll make a witness statement and then you can take a statement from him about his side of the incident.'

'You don't expect me to make a statement backing up what you say, do you?' Larkin demanded. 'The only talking I'll do will be to a lawyer. And get Strafford in here. He's my boss and I was on an errand for him when this big man-eater picked me up.'

'Lock him in a cell and we'll get down to it,' Carter said.

'I'll take your word on anything you say, Carter,

because you told me that you are a Texas Ranger.' Haskell gazed into Carter's face and Carter met his eyes, sensing keenly his brazen lie about his present status, but he felt that anything he could do to uncover local crookedness would be acceptable. The sheriff lowered his gaze. He seemed to be suffering some kind of conscience trouble. He grabbed Larkin by a shoulder. 'Come on, the cells are this way.' He thrust the prisoner along a passage blocked off by an iron door and used a key to unlock it. They entered the cell block.

Carter remained by the desk. He heard the clang of a door and a key grated in a lock.

'Don't forget I want a lawyer, and Strafford,' Larkin shouted.

Haskell came back into the office and tossed the cell keys on the desk. 'I'm gonna have to get a couple of new deputies,' he said, dropping into his seat.

'The ones you've got are useless.'

'I told you, I didn't hire them. But I'm gonna fire them.'

'Don't bother. When they are ready they'll make a play for me and I'll have to kill them. And that's the best way to get rid of their kind. Plant them six feet under on Boot Hill.'

'That's a helluva way to run the law.'

'If you've got a better way of handling them then I'll be pleased to hear it.' Carter leaned forward in his seat. 'Let's get my statement down. Then you can think over some questions I need to know the answers to.'

They became engrossed in getting Carter's statement on paper. The sheriff did the writing, and
frequently interrupted Carter to get at the exact
words he needed to use in order to give the court a
clear picture of the criminal act that Carter had witnessed. When they were both satisfied, Carter leaned
back in his seat and fixed Haskell with an intent gaze.

'I'm still trying to decide whether or not you are
an honest law man or just in the business to make
money and further the aims of disreputable men.'

Haskell reared up in his seat, a torrent of denial
issuing from his mouth. Carter held up a hand and
the sheriff lapsed into silence.

'Listen, Sheriff, I've had plenty of experience in
law dealing, and one thing I learned early in my
career was how to pick out bad men and tell with
some accuracy when they are lying. So, let's get down
to business. I'll ask questions and you answer them
truthfully. That way we'll make some progress. We
can talk about our differences later.'

'OK,' said Haskell, his eyes narrowed. His face was
taut and he looked uncomfortable, as if he had been
caught out in a lie.

'So, tell me about the bank robbery and how my
brother got mixed up in it.'

'It was a big shock to me when I went to the bank
after shots were fired, and Henry Maddock told me
he recognized your brother Nick as one of the
robbers. I thought I knew Nick quite well, and in my

book he was all right. But Maddock wouldn't have it. He recognized Nick, and so I had to treat your brother as a suspect. I sent out a posse with Swanson leading it, and when they returned I was told they caught up with the robbers and there was a shoot-out. Your brother was hit and seen to fall into the river and disappear. I've got statements to that effect.'

'I'll want the names of the posse men who accompanied Swanson.'

'Sure, but they all gave the same answer to what happened at the shoot-out.'

'I'll sort the chaff from the wheat later. Where did Burton, Milton and Swanson come from in the first place? Are they local men?'

'No. They were cowpokes, working for Strafford when I first saw them.'

Carter laughed and shook his head. 'I should have seen that coming, huh? OK, that clears up a lot of the trouble that's happened. I'll get round to your three deputies when I have a breathing space. Was any other robber identified after the bank robbery?'

'Nobody came forward to say.'

'And did anyone beside the banker name my brother?'

'No.'

'Have you any idea why Maddock wanted Nick dragged into the robbery?'

Haskell shook his head. 'It's beyond me.'

'So, did you give your deputies specific orders on

a day to day basis regarding their duties?'

'No. They sorted out what they would do between themselves. They knocked out the small crime around town.'

'And left all the big stuff on the range to go the way Strafford wanted, huh? So how did you spend your time as sheriff?'

'I was usually out on the range. There was always rustling to look into, and of course I had to collect back taxes and sort out disputes.'

Carter sat back in his seat, shaking his head.

'I get the picture,' he said. 'You're gonna have to turn over a new leaf if you hope to continue wearing the sheriff badge around here.'

'I've done nothing wrong where my job is concerned. I'll stick around for a spell and see how things pan out.'

Carter got to his feet and walked to the street door. He glanced back at the sheriff and saw he was staring at the top of his desk, his face set. Carter departed and went along the street to the livery barn to collect his horse. He set out for what was left of Nick's ranch, his mind burning with the question of what had happened to his brother. Such was the state of his mind he decided that Nick came first and everything else would have to wait.

He rode in to Nick's ranch and looked around for Jake Mortimer. There was no sign of the surviving cowpoke, and he rode around the yard to the bunk house, which was deserted. He was beginning to think that something bad had happened to the youngster when he heard a voice calling and looked round to see Mortimer emerging from the barn.

'Are you OK?' Carter demanded.

'Sure. I was holed up in the barn. You told me to keep an eye on the place and I reckoned the best way to do that was to keep quiet and watch for visitors. But it was a waste of time. No one showed up. Did you catch up with Larkin?'

'Yeah, he's in the jail now. I want to talk to you about the last couple of weeks here at the ranch. How was Nick? Was he worried about anything? Did he act any different to his normal self? Who came to see him? Did he have any trouble with anyone?'

'Nothing much happened at all. He gave us all the chance to leave if we thought it was getting too dangerous, but we decided to stick.' Mortimer's voice trailed off and he gulped. 'The others would still be alive if they had taken their time and pulled out.'

'They were good men, and we'll settle matters for them when we get the rights of it and take on the bad men who killed them.'

'I don't reckon I can go on,' Mortimer had trouble getting his words out and he could not meet Carter's gaze. 'I don't want to quit, but it seems hopeless, just you and me here now.'

Carter nodded. 'OK, if that's the way you feel. Let me know what Nick owes you and I'll pay you.'

'Thanks. Have you seen that rider over to the east?

It looks like Rough Milligan is coming from out of town.'

Carter swung around and caught the movement of a rider approaching. 'It looks like Milligan,' he mused. 'What's he doing out here? I spoke to him in town earlier this morning.'

'Milligan was around here a lot of times just a few weeks ago. Then he stopped coming. You'd better be careful with him. He's a wild man.'

'Thanks for the warning. Why don't you ride out now and make for town? I'll see you there and settle up with you.'

Mortimer nodded and turned away. Carter remained watching Milligan's approach. He heard Mortimer's departing hoofs but did not break his concentration, his thoughts running fast and deep. Where did Milligan fit into this business? Carter shrugged. There was only one way to find out.

Milligan was in no hurry. He let his mount pick its way into the yard; his eyes were focused on the ground ahead of him. But Carter saw him flicking glances to left and right and noticed that his right hand was close to the butt of his holstered pistol.

'I'm having a look around,' said Milligan, reining in a few feet from where Carter was waiting. 'It looks like Nick has got nothing left out here.'

'Did you see anything of Strafford or his crew on your way here?' Carter responded.

Milligan shook his head. His eyes were serious. 'I'll make a sweep out to the west and look around there before I call it a day. But before I go I want to tell you something. My closest friend on this range is your brother Nick.'

'They say he's dead.'

'His enemies say he's dead. You should listen to his friends.'

'And what do you say?'

'Nick is out at my place, and he's far from dead. When I told him that you were in the county he wanted to see you; so I'll take you out to my place later today.'

'Nick is alive?' Carter caught his breath as Milligan's words drove the coldness out of his chest. He kneed his horse in closer to Milligan and clutched at the man's sleeve. 'What happened to him?' he demanded. 'Was he in that bank raid?'

'The hell he was! They set him up. When the bank was hit they put a man in the gang who resembled Nick. He was masked, and later he was killed deliberately. They said he was Nick. But Nick had been at my place for several days before the robbery and after, recovering from a wound received in a gun trap on the range, and he's been there ever since.'

'Who set him up?'

'You've been mixing with them; the bad men running the crooked business. They've got the town believing Nick's guilty of bank robbery, and they have to shut Nick's mouth before he can start convincing the locals that he was set up.'

'Can I see him now?'

'There's nothing to stop you, except you'll have to be careful when you ride into my place. The range is being watched for Nick, and it's a certainty that you'll be watched closely now they know you're his brother. I reckon the way to handle it is for you to ride ahead and I'll trail you to keep the bad men off your neck.'

'It would be better if I rode into your place after sundown.' Carter's thoughts were leaping ahead. He was impatient to see Nick but did not want to jeopardize his brother's security.

Milligan nodded. 'I'll go along with that. I've got something to do now, but I'll be back in town around five. You saw the way I came into town earlier, so head out in the direction I came from. Go to Antelope Creek, about six miles out. Hide out there and wait for me. I'll show up in time to travel with you to see Nick.'

'Thanks.' Carter swung in his saddle and turned back toward town while Milligan rode off to the north.

The relief that gripped Carter was tremendous, and he looked around with fresh hope as he loped back to town. Nick was alive! The thought ran through his head repeatedly. But the sounds of rifle shots coming from ahead alerted him to reality and he drew his pistol. When he topped a rise, he reined in and gazed at two riders in the middle distance who were in the act of approaching a fallen rider. Carter recognized a riderless horse as the animal Mortimer had been riding. He lifted his gun when one of the two riders took aim at the figure on the grass and fired. The bullet struck the rider who was aiming to shoot Mortimer, who fell sideways out of his saddle.

The other rider jerked around and gazed up at the crest. He swung his pistol in Carter's direction and fired five shots that crackled about Carter. Before Carter could reply to the fusillade, the man swung his mount and rode into a depression. Carter spurred his horse and hit a gallop in pursuit. He passed Mortimer, now lying on his back in the lush grass. He saw blood on Mortimer's face. The man he had shot was on his back, with blood showing on his shirt front.

Carter saw the escaping man emerge from the depression and head for a tree line to the left. He spurred his mount and gave chase until the rider disappeared into them. He followed the line of trees to his right and swung left when he reached a gap cutting through them. A game trail headed into the thick of the trees and he followed it. When he heard a horse on his left crashing through a thicket, he reined in, drew his gun, and covered the area. A few moments later the rider he had been following emerged from cover and turned his horse to ride north. He didn't see Carter and reined in quickly when Carter fired a shot that almost creased his left ear. He glanced over his shoulder, saw Carter bearing down on him, and pulled his horse to a halt and raised his hands.

'Get down,' Carter ordered, reining in behind the

man. 'Trail your reins.' He stepped out of his saddle, his gun covering the man. 'Get rid of your gun and throw up your hands.'

'Is this a hold-up?' the man demanded.

'You know very well what it is. You and another cowpoke shot Jake Mortimer a few minutes ago. Don't say you weren't there because I got a good look of your horse before you fled, and I'd recognize that animal anywhere. What's your name?'

'You're making a big mistake. I'm Sime Bennard and I ride for Strafford's C Bar S ranch. I'm on my way to round up strays south of here.'

'Is that why you were riding north when you came out of that thicket? Tell me why you killed Mortimer.'

'I can see you won't believe me, whatever I say. Who are you, anyway, and what right have you to pull me up?'

'I'm Nick Carter's brother – his twin brother. You'd better start telling me the truth or I'll really get tough.'

'You ain't got a leg to stand on,' Bennard replied, leering, and Carter leaned sideways and struck him a blow to the head with the barrel of his pistol.

Bennard's legs crumpled and he dropped to the ground. Carter stood over him, gun levelled. But Bennard was out cold. Carter tethered both horses to a nearby branch and then squatted beside Bennard, rifled through his pockets, but found nothing of use. He sat back on his heels until Bennard began to stir, and then stood erect and toed him with his boot.

'It's time to rise,' Carter said harshly. 'I need some answers, and I'm mighty tired of waiting for someone to give me the right word. You're elected, Bennard, so don't make the mistake of trying to hold out on me.'

Bennard got unsteadily to his feet and stood rubbing his left temple, where contact with Carter's gun had raised a large bruise which was leaking drops of blood.

'Let's try again, huh?' Carter persisted. 'I'll ask some simple questions and all you have to do is answer truthfully. If you don't, I'll pistol-whip you. So why did you kill Mortimer? He didn't have any great part in whatever's going on around here. You killed him in cold blood.'

'I don't play a big part around here. I draw wages and do as I'm told. If you want to know what's going on, then you'll have to ask someone who has the answers.'

'So, give me the name of the man who told you to kill Jake Mortimer.'

'You've got a one-track mind, mister, and I can't answer any of your questions.'

Carter struck again with his gun and caught Bennard's right cheek which split the skin under the eye and caused a trickle of blood to appear. Bennard's knees buckled and he sank slowly to the ground. Carter stood back and waited.

'This could go on all day,' he said. 'I won't feel it, and I wouldn't want to be in your boots when I've finished with you.'

'Go to hell!' Bennard jerked out.

Carter lifted his gun to strike Bennard again when a shot crashed, and a bullet crackled past his head. He looked up quickly and saw three riders coming toward him along the game trail, Strafford in the lead, gun in hand and smoke drifting around his head. Carter dragged Bennard to his feet and held him as a shield against the newcomers. He cocked his gun and prepared to fight, aware that he had waited too long to lock horns with the men who really knew what was going on. . . .

SEVEN

Strafford's voice echoed through the trees as he shouted orders to his two riders. Both men came forward with levelled guns and moved in front of Strafford to shield him.

'He's the man I want dead,' Strafford shouted, pointing at Carter. 'Nail him now: a hundred dollars to the man who puts him down.'

'I told you who would get shot first if you started gun play,' Carter shouted. 'My first slug has got your name on it, Strafford.'

Carter let go his hold on Bennard and the man fell limply to the ground. Strafford turned his horse and started to ride back the way he had come. His two gun men remained where they were, guns in hand.

'You two better get out of here before the shooting starts,' Carter warned, 'or you'll be in the thick of it.'

'Talk's cheap,' replied one of them.

Carter fired a shot instantly, and the man who had spoken jerked and slid out of his saddle. The second man kicked his heels into his mount's flanks and dis-appeared into the trees. A moment later he began shooting at Carter from cover. Carter holstered his pistol and drew his Winchester from its saddle boot. Strafford was still retreating north along the game trail. Carter stood behind his horse. He jacked a shell into the breech of his rifle, closed the mechanism, and thrust the muzzle across his saddle to cover Strafford, who was still moving away. He aimed for Strafford's left shoulder. The rifle cracked sharply, and Strafford's heavy figure pitched sideways out of his saddle. Echoes of the shot faded quickly.

The rider who had fallen on the trail was unmov-ing, lying on his back with both hands at his sides. The second man was making a run for it through the trees, and Carter turned his attention to Strafford. He put away his rifle and drew his pistol again, swung back into his saddle and rode to where Strafford was lying on his belly, barely conscious, a bullet hole in his left shoulder. He turned his head and glared at Carter.

'You shot me in the back!' he exclaimed.

'I said you'd be my first mark if you caused trouble, and here you are raising hell, so you're down with a slug in you. Some men just can't see trouble ahead even if they tripped over it, and you've got a plateful now, Strafford.'

Carter checked Strafford for weapons, removed a pistol from the big rancher's holster and a back-up gun from an inside pocket. He turned the rancher onto his back and examined his wound. The bullet had struck high in the back, impacted on a bone and been turned upwards and out through the top of the shoulder. It looked messy, but Carter decided it was not serious. Strafford was built like a horse and would be better in a few weeks.

'Stop the bleeding,' Strafford rapped.

'Mister, you can lie there and bleed to death for all I care, but I want some answers, and you are going to tell me what I want to know.'

'What in hell are your questions? I ain't fit to answer anything right now. Get me back to my ranch or take me into town so the doctor can treat me. What kind of a man are you, for God-sakes?'

'Stop flapping your lip about your problem and listen to me. I want to know what you're up to. You sent a gunman to burn down my brother's ranch and kill off his crew.'

'What the hell are you talking about? I know nothing of that. I'm extending my ranch, but I'm paying hard cash for what I want.'

'You're lying, Strafford, but I'm wise to you. I'll give you a demonstration of how I treat liars when they don't give me straight answers.'

'What are you gonna do?'

Carter leaned over Strafford and raised his left fist. He punched sharply, his knuckles smacking into the bloody mess surrounding the wound in Strafford's shoulder. Strafford screamed like a woman as agony flared through his shoulder.

'Do you get the message?' Carter demanded. 'If you've got any sense you'll tell the truth to avoid more punishment.'

'You won't get away with this,' Strafford yelled. 'I'll see you dead for this.'

Carter punched the wounded shoulder again, his face expressionless, his eyes cold and watchful. Strafford yelled again in agony and thrashed about like a beetle that had fallen on its back. He tried to strike Carter who was just out of range, and Carter raised his left fist again, threatening to continue the punishment. Strafford fell silent and slumped. His eyes were closed, flickering.

'I'm waiting for an answer to my question,' said Carter in a low tone.

'What the hell can I tell you when I don't know anything about what's happening around here? I've got enough troubles on my plate without getting mixed up with local crooks.'

'You had my brother's ranch burned down and his crew killed,' said Carter implacably. 'That's all I'm interested in at the moment, so talk about that.'

'OK, I told my men to lean on your brother, to put some pressure on him to make him think about selling up. If I'd known he was a bank robber I could have saved myself a lot of trouble.'

Carter straightened and looked around. He didn't believe Strafford, but it sounded like the truth. He came to a sudden decision.

'I'll come back to you later, Strafford. I've got

other things to handle right now, and you'll keep.'

'Don't leave me here,' Strafford begged. 'I need help.'

'You can help yourself,' said Carter grimly. 'I'm thinking of the innocent cowpokes you had killed. Don't think you've got away with murder. I'll be back to deal with you when I get the time. I'm going back to town, and I'll tell the doctor you can be found at your ranch house. If you get there it will be under your own efforts.'

He untied his horse and swung into the saddle. Strafford begged and pleaded for help, but Carter rode away, his face impassive. He went back to where Jake Mortimer was lying. The young cowboy was dead. Carter placed him across the saddle of the horse standing nearby and started back for town, feeling strangely emotional, aware that the time for action had come and he had to start fighting, despite the fact that he was in the minority. . . .

Singletree was baking under a brassy sun burning in the cloudless sky when Carter saw it in the distance. He rode into the main street and dismounted outside the law office. The town looked as if all its inhabitants were asleep. A dog lying in the shade of a buckboard being loaded with supplies in front of the general store, lifted his head and opened one eye to check Carter's arrival, but dropped his head back on his paws, closed his eye and relaxed.

Carter wrapped his reins around a post, tethered Mortimer's horse, and stepped onto the sidewalk.

The door of the law office stood open to catch any breeze. Carter entered, and saw Sheriff Haskell seated at his desk, his head resting in his hands, eyes closed. Carter slammed the street door with enough force to make it sound like a clap of thunder. Haskell came up out of his seat like a startled antelope, reaching for his holstered gun. He dropped back into his chair when he recognized Carter.

'If you had any sense you'd be sitting in the shade somewhere,' Haskell said in a disgruntled tone.

'I've got Jake Mortimer outside, face-down across his saddle.'

'The hell you say!' Haskell straightened in his chair and gazed intently at Carter, trying to gauge his mood. 'What's been going on?'

'It's a fact that Strafford's crew are guilty of murder. I've left some of them dead on the range. Strafford turned up at the scene while I was there, and I put a shot through his shoulder. If you get a posse together you'll be able to pick him up. He'll be at his spread or trying to make his way there. Either way he's guilty of murder, and you'd better pick him up pronto.'

'I'll deal with it,' Haskell said, and settled back in his seat.

'Is Swanson still behind bars?' Carter demanded.

Haskell grimaced. 'Of course he is. You look done in, Carter. Why don't you cool off and relax? The trouble will still be here this evening.'

Carter turned to depart. He would get around to

Haskell in time, but right now he was concerned about his brother, and decided not to wait until nightfall before looking for Nick at Milligan's place. He had taken Milligan's word about his brother, but Milligan could have been lying through his teeth. He looked over his shoulder at the sheriff, saw him picking up a book to resume reading, and fought down the anger bubbling inside.

'Why don't you get Mortimer's body off the street?' he suggested.

'He's dead, ain't he? So he's past caring about the heat or anything. I'm being run off my feet since my three deputies have been put out of action. In fact, I'm waiting for a couple of likely prospects to show up for a chat, and I hope to engage them as deputies.'

Carter went out to the street. He took hold of the reins of Mortimer's horse, swung into his saddle, and rode along to the undertaker's establishment. The street door stood wide open. Carter wrinkled his nose at the smell of death that pervaded the place. He entered a front shop, heard someone using a saw on wood, and walked through to a back room.

A tall, thin man straightened and laid down his saw. He was past middle age. His whiskered face was cadaverous, his eyes dull. He looked like a man with no interest in anything but his job.

'I'm Bill Denton,' he said. 'You want something?'

'I've got Jake Mortimer outside, face-down on his horse. Take care of him for me. He worked for my brother, Nick Carter. I'll see you get paid for the job.

I'm Link Carter.'

'That's fine. There'll be no trouble. Have you informed the sheriff of Mr Mortimer's death and the circumstances surrounding it?'

'That's all been taken care of.'

'May I ask the circumstances of the death?'

'He was shot by two men riding for Strafford, the C Bar S rancher.'

'And does the sheriff know that?'

'Yeah, but it isn't worrying him at the moment. It will catch up with him later.'

Carter departed and rode along to the livery barn. Young Ryan Kelly emerged from the office inside the barn, and grinned when he saw Carter.

'I saw you riding along the street a while ago, and you had a dead man on the horse you were leading,' Kelly said. 'Has there been more trouble?'

'There'll be nothing but trouble until it has been stamped out,' Carter replied. 'Can you set me up with a good horse until tomorrow? I've got to ride out again shortly and my horse is on his last legs.'

'I'll do anything for you, Mr Carter.'

'How's your father doing?'

'He's settling down to resting until his wound is better, but he's mighty impatient. I'll get a good horse for you. Ma says you won't have to pay for any meal you eat in her diner.'

'That's good news. Your mother is the best cook around. Bring the horse outside. I'll be watching the street.'

'Are you expecting trouble?'

'I'm always on my guard for it, which is about the same thing. Don't worry about the trouble. It will blow over soon.'

Carter stood outside the barn and looked around the street. Kelly led Carter's horse into the barn. Carter saw Sheriff Haskell emerge from the law office, yawn, and look around. When he saw Carter at the livery barn Haskell went back into his office and closed the door. The sound of hoof beats on the trail made Carter glance over his shoulder. He stiffened when he saw two riders coming into town off the trail. He noticed that both horses were branded C Bar S. He dropped his right hand to the butt of his holstered pistol. Both riders stared at him in passing but kept riding along the street. Carter relaxed slightly when he saw them rein up in front of the doctor's house.

One of the riders dismounted, went to the doctor's door; and hammered on it. A middle-aged woman answered, and there was a lively discussion before the cowpoke turned away. When the two riders rode off they headed south and left the town. Kelly appeared leading another horse for Carter.

'This horse will outstay anything on the range,' Ryan said. 'He'll stay all day and run all night.'

'Those two riders on the point of riding out of town are mounted on C Bar S horses,' Carter said. 'What spreads lie out the way they are riding?'

'There's nothing much. Rough Milligan's horse

ranch is the other side of Antelope Creek, and one or two shoe-string ranches have set up in that direction.'

'Thanks for the mount. I'll see you when I get back.' Carter checked his cinch before swinging into the saddle and setting off along the street, following the two Big S riders. As he passed the jail, Sheriff Haskell opened the law office door and stepped out onto the sidewalk. He did not speak to Carter but remained watching him until he passed from view.

The two C Bar S riders hit a gallop as soon as they were out of town, and Carter touched spurs to his horse to keep them in sight. Two hours later, they were approaching a large creek. The riders passed along the right-hand side of the glinting water and swung off to the north-east. Carter remained on their trail like a faithful bloodhound. The men were following a faint trail that Carter guessed led to Milligan's place, and he closed in, loosening his pistol in his holster as he did so.

Several shots rang out, echoing swiftly, and Carter was plunged into furious action. The men Carter was following crossed a ridge at a gallop. Carter rode to the crest and reined in, looking around quickly. In the middle distance he saw a buckboard hurtling along the trail from a ranch headquarters in the background, and three riders were chasing it, their drawn guns blasting at the driver. Carter kicked his horse into movement and galloped into action. He recognized the driver of the wagon. It was Mrs Milligan.

The two men Carter was following reacted in different ways to the shooting. One rode hell for leather for the buckboard. The other whirled his horse and waited for Carter to ride over the crest. His gun was in his hand. He fired point blank at Carter, who ducked as a slug went through his hat brim. Carter had pulled his gun at the first sound of shooting. He cleared the crest in two bounds, and almost collided with the man attempting to shoot him.

His reaction was fast and lethal. He fired a shot and saw blood spurt from the man's shirt front. The man's horse reared, and its rider vacated his saddle in a low arc and crashed on the slope. Carter went on, urging his horse to greater effort, holding his reins in his left hand and preparing to tackle the second rider. In the background he heard more shooting.

The second rider twisted in his saddle and fired a shot at Carter, which missed, although Carter heard it crackle past his right ear. He fired in reply and the rider jerked and swayed in his saddle. Carter fired again, and the horse went down, throwing the rider out of leather. He passed them before they stopped slithering on the ground and spurred his horse to gain on the buckboard and its pursuing riders.

Carter could see Mrs Milligan in the driving seat of

the buckboard, using a whip, and he spotted a figure sitting in the back of the wagon, exchanging fire with the pursuers, who were gaining on the vehicle. He fully expected to see the buckboard overturn but somehow it stayed upright and kept moving at a tremendous pace. Carter urged his mount into a faster gait, and as soon as he was in range he began shooting at the pursuers. His first shot warned the men that they had unexpected company, and one of them whirled his horse around and came fast toward Carter, gun smoke flaring around him as he triggered his weapon.

With slugs snarling all about, Carter hunched lower in his saddle and lifted his pistol. He fired a single shot and a moment later the rider fell forward over the neck of his mount and then pitched to the ground. The other two riders turned instantly. Carter went on, watching for his chance. The buckboard continued at its breakneck pace and disappeared in a fold in the ground.

Carter lifted his Colt, fired a shot, and the left-hand rider vacated his saddle. The surviving man pulled on his reins and turned his horse away. The next instant he was high-tailing it, heading for cover. Carter reined in and swung his horse to chase the buckboard. He saw it in the distance, travelling as if it were making for the next county. He touched spurs to his mount and set off in pursuit.

When he drew within gun range, Carter lifted his hat and waved it over his head. He could see the face of the man in the back of the buckboard, and sunlight glinted on a rifle in his hands. The man was staring at him, and suddenly shouted to Mrs Milligan. Carter saw the woman turn her head and look at him, and then she was hauling on her reins and the buckboard slewed to a halt.

Carter holstered his pistol and rode to the buckboard. The man in the back was getting to his feet, and Carter felt a pang of emotion stab through him when he recognized his brother Nick, who was grinning. Mrs Milligan sat motionless on her seat, just watching.

'You're a hard man to run to ground, Nick,' Carter said, 'and you look like you've been fighting a bunch of wild cats.'

'Them and a lot more,' Nick replied. He looked exactly like his twin brother; same shape and colouring, and the same smile. He wore a thick bandage around his left shoulder. His face was pale, and he sat down suddenly, as if the strength had fled from his legs. 'I'm sure glad to see you, Link, but you took your sweet time getting here.'

'If I'd known you were in trouble I would have made haste. I didn't learn until today where you were hiding. So where are you heading now? Mrs Milligan was certainly laying on the whip.'

'Those three guys chasing us – Strafford's riders – turned up at the Milligan place and took us by surprise. We pulled out quick, and weren't heading any place in particular, but it looked like we wouldn't get far until you showed up. I am sure glad to see you, Link.'

'Not as glad as I am to see you, Nick. I had heard that you robbed a bank last week.'

'I hope you didn't believe it.'

'It never entered my head.'

'There's a set-up in town that will take some beating, and Strafford is grabbing all the range he can get his hands on. But he's not the only one causing trouble. There are others with their fingers in the pie. I've kept my eyes open and I've seen things. That was why they tried to frame me with the bank robbery. It's not gonna be easy to stop it, Link.'

'Strafford won't be troubling you much now. I put a slug through his shoulder and he ain't so eager to push his land-grabbing.' He smiled at Nick's expression. 'I'll explain the details later. Right now we'd better get you under cover again. I need you to fill me in on what's been going on around here, and who is crooked and who is not.'

Nick shook his head. 'Like I said, I know some of the men who are bad, but they are just small fry. The men running the crookedness have got themselves buried deep in the woodpile, and it's impossible to dig them out. But one thing is for sure, Link, that saloon-owner, Art Forder, is a dyed-in-the-wool bad man.'

'I know him from Texas,' Carter said. 'I ran him out of Renton. He's one of the first I'll set my sights on when we get to the final showdown. I've put two of the three deputies out of action.'

'You have been busy.' Nick smiled grimly. 'What do you make of Sheriff Haskell?'

'I haven't got him pegged yet. I'm real suspicious about him, and I reckon he'll show his true colours before we get through.'

'Let's go into town now and start shooting,' Nick suggested. 'I know where to start, and I'm itching to get my own back on those snakes. The banker, Henry Maddock, is crooked. He put a man in a gang of robbers posing as me, and that was to get me jailed so he could steal my ranch.'

'That's how I've got it figured, as far as it goes. Are you up to riding into town yet? You sure look pasty, as if a strong wind would blow you over.'

'I've been ready for some days. All I needed was a wake-up call to get moving. The shooting this morning has whetted my appetite for a showdown, and now I can't wait to get on with it.'

Carter turned his attention to Susan Milligan. 'What do you say, Mrs Milligan?'

'Don't start anything until my husband is on hand to help,' she replied.

'He'll be in town later, so he told me,' Carter said. 'There's no time like the present, so we'll ride into town and start the action.'

'I don't think Nick is ready for that yet,' Mrs Milligan said. 'Give him a few more days and then he'll be fit to flatten the town.'

'I'm ready now,' Nick said in a tone Carter knew well.

'So, let's go calling,' Carter urged.

Mrs Milligan drove the buckboard at a fast pace, as if she was impatient for the shooting to start. Nick sat in the buckboard with his back to the driving seat, hanging on with both hands, his pale face screwed up in an expression of pain. Carter rode beside the vehicle, watching their surroundings for hostility, and when he spotted movement on a crest to his right he called to Mrs Milligan to increase her pace.

They hammered into town from the south, and immediately became snared in the volume of traffic on Main Street. Mrs Milligan forced her way through the throng, easing her way into a space in front of the general store. Carter dismounted, and Nick climbed out of the buckboard. Mrs Milligan joined them on the sidewalk.

'You'd better take cover in the store,' Carter told her, and she hurried into the building without hesitation.

'Where do we go first?' Nick asked, drawing his pistol and checking its loads.

'There's only one place right now; the law office.' Carter caught a movement in the doorway of the store and dropped his hand to the butt of his pistol. A big figure loomed up out of the dim interior of the building – Brag Swanson – wearing two guns around his thick waist and a leering grin on his fleshy face.

'What are you doing out of jail, Swanson?' Carter demanded.

'What do you think?' Swanson planted his boots on the sidewalk and reached for his gun. . . .

EIGHT

Carter reacted to the situation the instant he saw Swanson and, when the big deputy made his play, he set his right hand into motion. His pistol came out of leather, thumb cocking the piece as it levelled, and Swanson's gun was still in his holster when Carter covered the deputy. Swanson cleared leather and opened his fingers in the same instant. His gun clattered on the sidewalk. He lifted his hands shoulder high, his face setting in a scowl.

'What changed your mind?' Carter demanded.

'You got me this time,' Swanson growled.

'If you want to try again you can pick up your gun.' Carter waited for a reply, but Swanson shook his head, and Carter asked:

'So, what are you doing out of jail?'

'Haskell turned me loose to help him with law dealing.'

'Head back to the jail, and if I see you on the street again I'll shoot you on sight.'

Swanson shrugged and walked along the sidewalk with Carter and Link following him. They entered the law office. Sheriff Haskell was at his desk, and his face showed annoyance when he saw Carter.

'I never get a minute to myself in this blamed job,' he commented. 'Now what is it?'

'I just picked up Swanson at the store,' Carter said flatly. 'How many times do I have to tell you that when I jail a man he stays jailed until I release him?'

'I've got no one else to run errands for me,' Haskell retorted. 'There ain't a man in town will pin on a deputy badge, and I can't handle this place on my own. OK, so the deputies I had were useless, but they were better than nothing.'

'Put Swanson back behind bars, and this time leave him there. What about the other prisoners? Where is your other ex-deputy – Burton?'

'He's in the cells, medically unfit for duty, thanks to you.' Haskell eyed the gun in Carter's hand, which was covering Swanson. Haskell glanced at the silent Nick Carter. 'So, you've turned up again, huh,' he observed.

'You knew he wasn't dead!' Carter said. 'Get up off your chair and put Swanson back behind bars. I've got serious doubts about you, Sheriff. Who are the crooked men in town who organized the bank robbery? It's time they were in jail.'

'If I knew who they were they would be sitting in the cells right now,' Haskell said.

'Let's take a walk,' Nick cut in. 'I know some of the

111

men involved in the robbery, and it's time we tried our luck with them.'

Carter nodded, and they left the office and paused on the sidewalk. Nick closed the office door, but it was opened instantly from the inside. Carter looked around quickly, and saw Haskell confronting him, a pistol in his hand.

'Hold it, you two,' the sheriff said sharply, covering them with his gun. 'This is my town and I sure as hell don't want more trouble cropping up because you're nosing around. Lift your hands and I'll draw your teeth. Then you can see the inside of my jail.'

'You're making a big mistake, Sheriff,' Carter said. He looked into the barrel of the sheriff's gun and realized that he had no chance of gaining the upper hand.

'No. You made the mistake of trying to take over the law hereabouts. You lied to me about being a Texas Ranger. I sent a wire to Ranger Headquarters in Austin and their reply got here this afternoon. You quit the Rangers weeks ago and have no legal standing now. So, some of the killings you've done around here may be illegal and if so, you'll face charges of murder. Stand still now and Swanson will take your gun.'

Swanson emerged from the law office, grinning, and took their pistols. They were escorted into the jail and locked in a special cell away from the main cells. Haskell holstered his gun when the jail door had been locked.

'I'll get around to you two later. Be prepared for a long stay behind bars because I've got a lot of checking up to do. And don't give me any trouble. I'll come down hard on you for the slightest misdemeanour.'

'Who are you working with, Haskell?' Carter demanded. 'Is it Maddock, Strafford, or Art Forder?'

'You're loco if you think I'm crooked. I'm the law, and I'll enforce it no matter who I come up against. Come on, Swanson, we've got work to do. I want statements from Burton about the rights of the shooting they were involved in with Carter.'

Swanson chuckled. 'Burton couldn't tell the truth if he wanted to,' he opined.

Carter sat down on a bunk in the cell as Haskell departed followed by Swanson. Nick joined him, stifling a groan as a half-healed wound in his back complained at the action.

'Looks like we got bad trouble on our hands, Link,' Nick observed. 'I always thought Haskell was a straight guy but putting you in jail sure throws a different light on him. What do we do now? My experience warns me to get out of here but quick. The bunch that hit the bank was pretty slick and I was dragged into that business like a two-year-old steer being roped for branding. The first time I knew anything about my part in it was when a couple of men held me up in an alley. One of them hit me in the chest with a slug, but I killed him and bored the other through the shoulder. I was on the run until

Rough Milligan found me and took me out to his place. In between I was attacked by Strafford's men, and when I got away from them I came up against those deputies, Swanson, Burton and Milton.'

'And you can't tell me who is bossing the trouble?'

Nick shook his head. 'I was getting more than my share of trouble from Strafford. I figured he was after my spread, and I had my work cut out trying to fight him off. He's got nigh on thirty men on his payroll, and at one time they were coming at me from all directions. And you mentioned the banker and that saloon owner, Art Forder. You've got pretty close to the mark, Link.'

'Not close enough. We've got to get out of here, but fast. When word gets out that we're in jail there's no telling what will happen.'

'You're the law man in the family, so what do you think?'

'Give me a little time and I'll come up with something. But I've got some bad news for you, Nick. All your crew are dead. Strafford's men accounted for them, so we know what to do when we finally bring Strafford to book.'

'So how do we get out of here?' Nick demanded.

'We'll get out or die in the attempt,' Carter said grimly. 'We'll make a play to escape the first time Haskell or Swanson comes back in here.'

'We certainly walked into trouble, riding into town like we did.' Nick rubbed his chin, his eyes filled with speculation. 'I don't have one friend in this burg,

114

and I don't suppose you had time to meet anyone. I learned a long time ago that I was on to a hiding to nothing, but I couldn't give up.'

'Who is talking of giving up?' Carter grinned. 'Never say die, Nick. We've got a lot going for us.'

He walked to a barred window that overlooked the back yard of the jail. It was large, and gallows were built in a corner. Nick joined him, and they studied the grim scene. Nick tested the bars by shaking them, and although they creaked, were firmly fixed.

'We'll go out by the front door when we leave,' Carter said. 'Sit down and get some rest. You'll need your strength when we do get out; you look ready to drop.'

Nick nodded and stretched out on a bunk. He closed his eyes and slowly relaxed into sleep. Carter studied his brother's face before turning his thoughts to the situation. He made a detailed search of the big cell, looking for any weakness that would give them an opportunity to break out.

He found nothing that could help him and sat down on the other bunk to think over his problems. From what he had seen and done since his arrival, he had accepted that there were three men who were likely to be involved in the trouble – Art Forder the saloon man, Henry Maddock the banker, and Strafford the rancher. He was certain of Strafford's guilt; had proof the rancher was guilty of murder. He suspected Henry Maddock of master-minding the robbery on his bank and being involved in framing

Nick. Art Forder was a different problem. The saloon man had a record of crookedness in Texas, and he was the type to plunge into local illegalities, given the opportunity. Then there was Haskell. The sheriff was an enigma. His actions suggested that he was not honest, but there was no proof against him – yet.

Turning his attention to the question of escaping, he fancied he should overpower the next man to unlock their cell, and mentally prepared himself for that eventuality. Believing that action was paramount, he went to the door of the cell and called for the sheriff. Some minutes elapsed before Haskell appeared.

'I haven't eaten today, Sheriff. Get someone to go along to Mrs Kelly's diner and ask her to bring two meals in here. Tell her they are for me – she's promised me free meals while I'm in town and I might as well take advantage of her offer.'

'We have meals supplied for prisoners from the saloon kitchen at regular times. What's wrong with them?'

'I ate at Mrs Kelly's last night, and I like her food. And before you leave, how long are you gonna keep me cooped up in here?'

'I'm investigating the shootings that have occurred in town since you got here, and like I told you, if you're no longer a Texas Ranger, then you could be guilty of unlawful killing. You'll have to be patient. It will take me some days before I can be certain of your guilt or innocence.'

'I was pursuing certain lines of enquiry before you slammed the door on me, and if I don't follow them up immediately then they could fold on me.'

'So, what do you want me to do – let you out?' Haskell grinned and departed but paused at the door of the office and looked over his shoulder. 'I'll see about your food this once, but after today you'll eat when the rest of the prisoners do.'

Carter grimaced as he looked around the cell. He felt hemmed in by the confining walls, and his mind seemed to be hogtied. An hour passed, and the sheriff did not return. Carter chafed at the loss of time. He needed to be out there getting proof and felt like a deer with one foot caught in a trap.

When he heard the street door of the office slam and then loud voices, he became animated. The door to the cells was opened and Haskell stuck his head in to check on his special prisoners.

'Your grub is here,' Haskell said, and went back into his office.

The sound of metal cans clashing echoed through the jail, and then Ryan Kelly appeared in the doorway, carrying a stack of meal cans. He paused, looked around the cell, and then gazed at Carter. He came to the metal door of the cell and passed the cans through the horizontal slot in the vertical bars.

'I was shocked to hear you'd been jailed,' Kelly said in a half-whisper. 'Ma came to the stable and told me the sheriff had dropped by the diner and ordered two meals for you and your brother Nick.

So, Nick wasn't killed robbing the bank. What's going on? Is there anything I can do to help?'

Carter glanced at the half-open connecting door. He could hear Haskell's voice in the office. He lowered his voice.

'I need to get out of here, Ryan. Have you got a gun on you?'

Kelly's face changed expression. 'Do you want me to help bust you out?'

'No. All you've got to do is pass me a loaded pistol.'

'There's one in the bigger can. Ma insisted on putting it in. You better grab it before Haskell comes in.'

Carter opened the can and took out a .38 pistol. He watched the connecting door as he thrust the gun into the back of his belt. Kelly grinned.

'I'll come back later for the meal cans,' he said. 'You'd better drink the coffee now. It always gets cold before the food. Good luck.' He turned and walked back into the office.

Carter called Nick, who was sleeping. 'Come and get it. We'll move out after we've eaten.'

'What happened?' Nick demanded as he got off his bunk and took one of the meal cans.

'Eat first,' Carter said.

Haskell came into the cells later, accompanied by Ryan Kelly, who collected the cans and departed. The sheriff leaned against the barred door.

'I've been thinking,' he said. 'You did some good

work around here, Carter. Perhaps I was a bit hasty throwing you in a cell. I could do with some help, but I'll only release you if you promise to follow my orders.'

'What are you dreaming up now?' Carter demanded. 'Who have you talked to? I reckon you want to turn us loose to give the local hard-cases a chance to kill us. No chance, Sheriff. I'm wise to all the tricks in the book.'

Haskell turned on his heel and departed. Nick grinned.

'We've still got to get out of here,' he reminded. 'What's your plan?'

'We'll take it as it comes, Nick. I've decided to wait until after sundown – not so many folks around then.'

'Anything you say.' Nick shrugged. 'You're smarter than me.'

Swanson came to the cell an hour later. He was heavily armed, with crossed gun belts around his waist and two .45s in the holsters.

'Where's the war, Swanson?' Nick demanded.

'Right here in town. I've been in Forder's saloon. There was a rumour that certain men are planning to get rid of you two by lynching. They're likkering up like there's no tomorrow, and they're beginning to get noisy. Forder is handing out free drinks, and Henry Maddock, the banker, is there egging the crowd on; nagging about the way an honest bank teller was shot in cold blood.' He glanced at Nick.

'He's still insisting that you were one of the gang, even though it's been proved you weren't in on that job. But that don't matter a cuss. The mob will be coming this way before long.'

'Then you'd better get us out of here damn quick, Swanson. Only a fool would take chances with a lynch mob howling for blood.' Nick gripped the bars of the cell. 'I witnessed a lynching once, and I don't want to see another.'

'You won't see much of this one,' Swanson replied with a grin. 'You're the one who's gonna swing.'

'Turn us loose so we can defend ourselves, Swanson,' Carter said.

'Not me. Lynching you two will be good. We won't have to fool around getting rid of you ourselves.'

'So, you're admitting that the local law department want to get rid of us, huh?' Carter asked.

'Yeah, you won't be around to complain afterwards.' Swanson grinned. 'With you two dead, we'll be able to get back to our own way of working.'

'That includes Burton, huh?' Carter persisted.

'You got it in one.' Swanson smirked. 'We're leaving the jail deserted so the lynch party can get on with their work. They'll be along here shortly. So long, fellers!'

Swanson turned swiftly and departed. They heard the street door open and then slam. Silence ensued.

'It looks like they've got us in a bag,' Nick observed, 'and time is running out.'

'We need someone who has a cell door key,' Carter

replied grimly, 'and all we've got is a .38 pistol and five cartridges.'

'Don't waste any,' countered Nick, and grinned harshly.

The street door opened, and a voice called. 'Hey, sheriff, are you around? You've got trouble coming. There's a lynch mob gathered in Forder's saloon, and they'll be heading this way in a couple of minutes. You'd better get your prisoners out of here.'

'Come through to the cells,' Carter shouted, and then a man appeared in the doorway to the cells.

'Where's the sheriff?' he demanded. 'He'd better get you two out of here before hell breaks loose. That mob in the saloon is talking up a neck-tie party, and they've just about swallowed enough whiskey to handle the job.'

'There's no one here,' Carter said. 'Take a look in the office – on the desk or in the top right-hand drawer. Find the cell keys. Unlock this door and give us a chance to get away. We haven't done anything to put lynch ropes around our necks, so act quickly and prevent a serious injustice.'

'I don't need to be told that,' the man said. 'I'm aware of what you've done around here in the past few days.' He turned on his heel and went back into the office.

Carter could hear him opening a drawer, and at the same time he heard a frightening sound coming from along the street. A crowd of whiskey-inflamed men were on the march, howling and yelling, and the sound rapidly became louder; was punctuated by an occasional shot. Carter gritted his teeth as the words the mob were chanting came loud and clear.

'Hang 'em high! Hang 'em high! Hang 'em high!'

NINE

The man looking for the cell keys in the office came back into the cell block, his face showing fear. The chanting mob was coming noisily nearer along the street.

'I can't find the cell keys anywhere. I reckon one of the deputies has handed them to the mob. They can't hang you unless they can open the door of your cell.'

'Thanks for the try,' Carter said. 'You'd better get out of here, quick.'

'Good luck,' the man called. 'I'll leave by the back door. I wouldn't want to face that mob, the mood they're in.'

He moved away quickly, and the next moment he had gone. Carter drew the .38 Kelly had given him and checked the cylinder before returning the weapon to the back of his waistband.

'Don't get in my way when they come in here, Nick,' he said. 'If I can get the drop on them then you grab a gun and join in, huh? Don't pussy-foot with them. They're a lawless mob intent on hanging two innocent men.'

'And what is worse,' Nick replied, 'is that we are the two innocent men in question. I'm right with you, Link.'

They stood in silence, listening to the approach of the mob. The street door was thrown open with a crash, and boots thudded on the wooden floor as the mob surged to the cells. A press of men appeared in the doorway to the cells and fought each other to be the first to enter. They were under the influence of the whiskey they had imbibed, and all carried guns. They rushed the cell door where Link and Nick stood motionless, and were temporarily bewildered by the fact that it was locked.

'Where's the key?' demanded several voices in unison.

'It'll be in the front office,' someone suggested, and there was a general stampede out of the cell block.

Hank Maddock, the banker, remained in front of the cell, gazing at Carter like a cougar confronting its prey.

'So, you've come into the open at last, huh,' Carter observed. 'You're running this hanging party.'

'A teller was killed in the robbery,' Maddock said, 'and I want justice for him.'

'Do you call lynching justice?' Carter demanded. 'I have proof that Nick was set up in that robbery.

There are witnesses who know he was already wounded at the time. But you've got a different reason why you want him dead and buried. Why don't you tell us what it is?'

The men who had gone back into the law office returned, and one of them was waving a bunch of keys. There was a heavy silence while the keys were tried one by one without success, until the lock clicked, and the cell door was pushed open. Someone cheered, and the door was thrust open and men rushed into the cell. Nick was seized, but he went down fighting. Carter drew his gun and cocked it, backing into a corner of the cell. He fired a shot into the ceiling and men froze instantly.

'Get out of here, all of you,' Carter shouted, 'or I'll start killing.'

Someone swung a gun in Carter's direction. He fired instantly, and the man screeched and fell heavily, taking down two other men. Another produced a pistol and waved it in Carter's face. Carter snatched the gun and kneed the man, dropping him. He fired another shot into the ceiling. Men began moving out, but one reached for his holstered gun and turned to face Carter, who triggered another shot, aiming for the man's right thigh. The man yelled and fell to the floor, his gun still in his holster. Carter emptied one gun into the ceiling, dropped it, and snatched the weapon belted around the fallen man's waist. He menaced the crowd with two weapons. He heard an isolated shot, and looked over to where Nick was standing, holding a .45 with a curl of smoke rising from its muzzle.

'Get the hell out of here,' shouted Nick, and fired again, aiming above the heads of the would-be lynch party. The cell emptied slowly, and such was Carter's reputation in the town that no one was prepared to confront him.

'Keep going until you reach the street,' Carter rapped. 'Anyone I see out there when I have this place under control will find himself back inside on the wrong side of the bars. Nick, hang on to Maddock. We've got some business with him.'

Carter could feel sweat running down his face as the cell emptied and the would-be lynch-party departed, taking their wounded with them. The cell keys were swinging from the key in the lock. Carter went forward and took them. He stuck one of his guns into his waistband.

Boots thudded on the boards of the office, and then there was silence. Carter went through quickly to the front office, crossed to the street door and locked it. Nick came out of the cells. He held out his hand for the cell keys.

'I'll lock Maddock in a cell until you've got time to handle him.'

Carter gave him the keys.

'Arm yourself, Nick. It looks like there's no law around here now, so we'll take over until folks can get organized. You stay here and guard the prisoners while I go to the saloon and find out what part Art

Forder has played in this game.'

'I'd rather go along with you, Link,' Nick said.

'It can't be done. We've got to maintain control in town until the bad men are behind bars. Let's do it my way, huh?'

Nick nodded and examined the weapons in the gun rack in the office. Their gun belts were hanging on hooks, and Carter was relieved to find his own pistol in its holster.

'Keep the street door locked while I'm gone, and I'll sing out when I get back, hopefully with some prisoners,' said Carter as he moved to the street door and opened it cautiously. He half-expected to be met by a hail of gunfire but the street in front of the jail was deserted. Nick closed the door when Carter moved out to the sidewalk, and Carter heard the door being locked and bolted.

Shadows had closed in on Main Street, and a breeze was blowing in from out of town, bearing in its cooling breath the scents and smells of the great outdoors. Carter turned his face towards Art Forder's saloon, aware that he was thirsty, and the thought of a cold beer enlivened his desire. He walked along the side walk, sensing the loneliness around him, and he was certain that hidden eyes were watching his progress along the street. He was suddenly aware that the usual gridlock of wagons was absent. Not one ore wagon was grinding its way to the stamp mills on the other side of town. Instead of being relieved, he felt a menace in the atmosphere.

The saloon was silent inside. The usual nonstop sound of the old piano was missing. Carter paused at the batwings, his right hand down at his side, ready to draw his deadly gun at the first sign of hostility. He looked inside the saloon. A few men were at the bar with drinks before them, although no one was now drinking seriously, and card players sat at one of the tables with three men standing close by in rapt attention of the game in progress.

Carter pushed open the batwings with his left hand and crossed the threshold to walk to the bar. He looked around for Art Forder, but the proprietor was not in the big room. A bar tender came to him and Carter ordered a glass of root beer, which came sliding towards him on the polished surface of the bar.

'That's on the house,' Carter rasped.

'Yes, sir.' The tender was short and fat, middle-aged, his hair slicked down and parted in the middle; face pale and expressing tension. 'Mr Forder told me yesterday that you don't have to pay for anything while you're in here.'

'Where is Forder?'

'He's busy in his office.'

'Tell him I'm in the saloon and I want him out here to talk.'

'I'll tell him at once.' The bar tender scuttled to the far end of the bar and hurried to the office at the rear of the saloon. The silence was intense. Carter raised his glass and took a long gulp of the beer. He did not stop until the glass was empty, and the refreshment it afforded him was deeply satisfying.

The bar tender came scurrying back. 'Mr Forder said he'll be along in a minute, sir. I see you've finished your beer. Would you like another?'

'Thanks, but not right now. You're not very busy. Is it because the lynching failed?'

'What lynching?' The bar tender paused, and then shrugged. 'That's the way it goes in this business,' he said in a lower tone. He produced a handkerchief and mopped his sweating face.

Forder appeared at the far end of the bar. Carter looked at the bar tender and held his gaze.

'While I'm talking to Forder, don't let your hands leave the top of the bar. If you do, I'll kill you.'

The bar tender gulped, opened his mouth to reply, and then closed it again. He slapped hands palms down on the counter, and they looked as if they'd been nailed there.

Carter walked along the bar to where Forder was standing. The big saloon owner was smiling, but his face looked as if he had been sick all day. He called to the tender.

'I'll have a whiskey, Barney. Give Mr Carter whatever he wants.'

'So, the lynch party failed,' Carter said.

'I hope you're not thinking I had anything to do with it,' Forder said. 'I don't forget the favour you did for me back in Texas. I was against the lynch crowd in here, but there was nothing I could do about it.'

'Who planned it?' Carter's voice was little more than a whisper, but it was filled with hostility and menace.

Forder shrugged. His big face was free of expression, like a gambler's when he was dealing cards. He moved his feet tensely, shaking his head as he considered.

'You know I can't say anything about that. I'd be dead in the street in the morning if I said anything. You know already, I guess, who is back of it. All I can tell you is that Henry Maddock was in here earlier, buying drinks for everyone and egging them on to walk down to the jail with a rope. Two names were being mentioned for the hanging – yours and your brother's. Need I say more?'

'Maddock is in jail now. So, you haven't got into bad business, huh? You don't have any partners in town?'

'I told you, I'm strictly on the narrow. I learned my lesson in Texas.'

'A leopard doesn't change its spots, Forder. If I find out you're trying to fool me I won't run you out of town next time with your tail between your legs, I'll come gunning for you, and that'll mean a one-way ticket to Boot Hill.'

'I'm clean as a new-born baby, Carter. Why would I want to lynch you? I'm grateful to you for pulling me up short when I was ruining my life.'

'Were any of Strafford's crew involved in the trouble at the jail?'

Forder hesitated, and glanced around to check if he could be overheard. He moistened his lips and heaved a sigh. 'Strafford's ranch foreman, Frank Bullard, was in here while Maddock was getting a mob worked up. He left just before the mob headed for the jail. I overheard Bullard talking to someone, and Larkin's name was mentioned. You've got Larkin in jail now for killing your brother's crew, huh? Enough said.'

'I'll believe you for the moment, Forder,' Carter said. 'I hope for your sake that you're telling the truth. If you are lying to me then you better be gone from the town by sunup.'

'I'm not involved in anything crooked. I swear it. I wish you good luck, Carter.'

'I'll need plenty of luck,' Carter responded, heading for the door.

He took a deep breath when he was standing on the sidewalk outside the saloon. The evening shadows had thickened, and lamps were alight in some of the buildings. He glanced around the street, looking for signs of impending trouble, and glanced along the street towards the law office. The town was quiet, but had a brooding atmosphere, as if the trouble that had passed had left a dark shadow as a portent of worse things to come.

He checked the opposite side of the street, looking at the entrances to the several alleys cutting through from the main street to the back lots. He caught a quick movement in the alley between the gun shop and the butcher's, and moved instinctively, stepping to his left and dropping to one knee. A gun blasted, and a bullet hammered into the front of the saloon. Carter threw himself full length and palmed his gun.

Gun echoes thundered along the street. The hidden gun fired again, sending several slugs on a quest for Carter's flesh. He saw gun flashes from the alley, levelled his own, and returned fire, his aim unhurried but deadly. Gun smoke blew back into his face and he narrowed his eyes. He fired instinctively when he saw a shoulder and a hand holding the pistol, and saw the weapon flip out of the ambusher's grasp. He sprang to his feet instantly and ran across the street, heading for the alley mouth.

He dived across the opposite sidewalk and slithered into the alley, gun uplifted, finger tensed on the trigger. He saw a man in the act of getting to his feet, reaching for his gun lying in the dust. Carter fired a shot which struck the discarded pistol and sent it skittering several feet into the alley. The man straightened and turned to face Carter, his right hand going into his pocket. Carter saw a small gun appearing and triggered a shot that struck the ambusher's right forearm. The man fell to his knees and stayed there. Blood dripped from his wound and spattered the dust.

'Get up,' Carter ordered. 'What's your name?'

'I'm Todd Harman.'

'I've heard you were trying to find a gunman to

help you shoot me. You work for Art Forder, don't you? Who paid you five hundred bucks to kill me?'

Harman snarled and got to his feet. He was tall, muscular, in his early twenties, and had straw coloured hair that was long and straggly. He wore a long moustache that needed trimming. His face was contorted with pain, his eyes like those of a trapped bear.

'You'd better get me to a doctor before I bleed to death,' he rasped.

'You can bleed to death right where you're standing,' Carter retorted. 'Answer my questions and then you can see the doctor.'

Harman staggered, moved forward several steps, and his shoulders went forward as he dropped to the ground. He fell on his face and a tremor passed through him. Carter looked at Harman's wound and saw a great deal of blood. It looked like an artery had been cut by the bullet he had received. Carter holstered his gun and turned Harman onto his back, stripped the neckerchief from him and bound it around the upper right arm. He pulled it tight and knotted it, and the flow of blood lessened.

Carter straightened and looked around. He saw Art Forder peering at him from the batwings of the saloon and beckoned to him. Forder came, his face filled with question.

'Who is he?' Forder demanded.

'It's your man, Harman. Get the doctor, but fast. We'll talk later about this.'

Forder turned and ran along the street. Carter stood waiting for his return, thoughts welling up in his mind like water out of a mountain spring. Minutes later, Forder returned with a tall young man who was carrying a medical bag.

'This is Doc Lyndon,' Forder introduced, 'and this is Carter, the Texas Ranger, who's cleaning up the town.'

'We've met,' Carter said, and Lyndon nodded a greeting, but his attention was on Harman. He dropped to one knee, checked the wound and the rough tourniquet, and got to his feet.

'Let's get him into my office,' he said. 'I'll have to do some stitching before I'll loosen the tourniquet.'

'Help the doctor, Forder,' Carter said. 'I'm busy right now.'

He left the alley and went to the law office. The street door was locked. Lamplight showed at the front window, but Nick did not answer Carter's knock.

'Hey, Nick, come on. Open up.'

There was no reply. Carter turned the handle and then threw his weight against the door, which barely tremored under the assault. He guessed that some kind of trouble had hit his brother and went to the alley and passed along to the back of the jail, recalling the man who had tried to get them out of the cells when the lynch party was arriving and had left by the back door. He found the door unlocked, drew his gun, and entered the dimly-lit cells.

The place was deserted. There were no prisoners, and no sign of Nick. He went into the front office, also deserted, and found a pistol on the floor. He picked it up. It had not been fired. He wondered what had happened to his brother. Someone must have got the drop on him, but how? Nick knew enough not to be tricked into unlocking the street door. He looked at the lock on the door and saw that the keys were missing. He looked around but they were nowhere to be seen.

Carter feared that Nick would be hanged summarily and left the office and went back to the street. He listened intently for sounds that would indicate the presence of dangerous men and a prisoner. Nick would surely be calling for help, knowing that Carter was somewhere in town – unless his captors had rendered him unconscious.

He heard running feet coming towards him and drew his pistol. A figure appeared in the growing darkness, and he recognized Ryan Kelly, who came to him, breathing hard.

'It's your brother Nick,' Kelly gasped. 'Some of Strafford's crew sneaked into town. Strafford's ramrod, Frank Bullard, met them at the stable. I hid away when they appeared, and Bullard talked about grabbing Nick out of the jail and taking him out to Strafford's spread. They're going to force him to sign his ranch over to Strafford, and then they'll kill him. They went to the jail and came back to the stable with Nick, piled him on a horse, and took off for

Strafford's place.'

'I need a horse,' Carter said, and they both started running towards the stable.

'I got something else to tell you,' Kelly gasped as they continued. 'Can you guess who came and spoke to Frank Bullard while he was waiting for his crew to show up?'

'I ain't good at guessing games,' Carter replied. 'Give me a name.'

'Cassie Canfield – she sings in Art Forder's saloon. She came into the barn just after Bullard arrived, and talked to him like he was an old friend. I couldn't hear much of what she said because her voice was low, but she was giving him a message from Forder to pass on to Strafford, something about going easy because you were playing up hell with their main game.'

'I reckoned Forder was mixed up in this some-where,' Carter mused. 'I'll get back to him later. Right now, I've got to get after Nick before they kill him.'

They went into the stable and Kelly prepared a horse for travel.

'How do I find Strafford's spread,' Carter asked.

'You can't miss it if you take the north trail, which goes right past the ranch. It's about twelve miles out, and there's a big board at a left-hand fork with Strafford's name and brand on it.'

Carter nodded and swung into the saddle. He lifted a hand to Kelly, left the stable, and then used his spurs to hit a gallop. He sped out of town. Evening was drawing in. The sun was far over to the west and preparing to drop below the horizon. The empty trail was before him, and his brother was somewhere out here, friendless and facing great danger. . . .

TEN

Carter pushed his mount, his face set in determined lines, his mind set with the problem facing him. He had to get Nick away from Strafford. Time seemed to stand still as he continued, and it seemed a long, long time before he reached the left fork with the painted sign for Strafford's ranch. He slowed his pace as he turned off the main trail. It was obvious that Strafford would have guards around his spread if he was breaking the law.

He topped a rise and reined in; found himself staring down a slope at a ranch house that was ablaze with lamp light. He could see a line of saddle mounts tied up in front of the porch, and figures were moving around. A group of four men were standing on the porch near the open front door, and Carter clenched his teeth when he recognized Nick huddled before the massive figure of Strafford. The other two men were holding drawn guns, covering Nick.

Carter rode slowly down the slope towards the

ranch. He dismounted in a copse in a gully the quarter part of a mile from the house, drew his Winchester and left the horse under cover. He went forward quietly but swiftly. The lamp light issuing from the windows of the ranch house illuminated the close area around the building. Carter saw a mounted guard at the gate and slid into cover. He circled the ranch house and sneaked in closer from a point near the right front corner of the building, finding shadows in the undulations of the ground to conceal his presence.

He paused when he was at the corner and leaned sideways carefully until he could view the porch and the figures on it. Strafford was talking loudly and gesticulating, making points in his usual bullying way.

'You've got no chance this minute, Carter,' he was saying to Nick, who was constrained by the two pistols covering him. 'Give me a bill of sale for your spread and I'll pay you a fair market price. You'll be able to ride out of here before sunup and head for a new life some other place.'

'I wouldn't trust you if you were hog-tied in your saddle,' Nick replied. 'You and Maddock framed me with the bank robbery when I'd already been shot by one of your men and was hiding out on the range. I've told you all along that my future is right here, and hell and high water couldn't make me give up.'

'You'll change your mind before I get through with you,' said Strafford confidently. He turned to the bigger of the two men holding guns on Nick.

139

'Frank, you did real good in town. Keep Carter safe in the bunk house while you go back to town and get his brother – that hellion of a Texas Ranger. You're the only man I can rely on in this outfit, and when you catch Carter's brother, I want him hanged in a prominent place in town as a warning to anyone else who thinks he can get the better of me. Then find out what's happened to Sheriff Haskell. I need him back doing his duty.'

'Right, Boss, I'll head back to town right now. I'll take Wardell with me, just in case the big Texas Ranger gets out of hand.'

Carter eased back behind the corner. He heard boots scuffing the porch boards and eased sideways again, to see Bullard and Wardell taking Nick across the yard in the direction of the bunk house. There were riders at the corral, taking the saddles and gear off their mounts, and Carter could guess at the trouble he would have trying to get his brother out of the bunk house when all the crew had retired there.

He drew his pistol and stepped onto the porch. Strafford had entered the house and the front door was closed. He moved along to the door; it opened to his touch. He stepped inside, directly into the big living room, and caught Strafford in the act of removing his gun belt. The rancher heard the door closing and swung round, his expression changing when he saw Carter.

'Drop the gun belt,' Carter rapped, 'and come

over here to the door. Tell that ramrod you've changed your mind about my brother. You want him in here with you, and none of your crew is to leave the ranch until sunup.'

'Are you loco? I'd die before doing that.'

Carter cocked his gun. 'Where do you want it?' he demanded. 'You're standing right on the edge. Do like you're told or collect a slug dead centre.'

Strafford paused for the merest instant, and then dropped his gun belt. He came towards Carter reluctantly.

'There's no option for you, Strafford. Open the door and call your ramrod to bring my brother back here. If you make a mistake and try something, then you're dead.'

Strafford nodded and opened the door. 'Hey, Bullard,' he shouted. 'I've changed my mind. Bring Carter back here and forget about riding out tonight. We'll go into town at sunup.'

Carter touched the back of Strafford's bull neck with the muzzle of his pistol. He drew his spare gun and emptied the cylinder.

'You're doing real good,' he said. 'Take this empty gun and cover my brother with it. Do it right and there's a good chance you'll see tomorrow's sunup.'

Bullard came back across the yard, moaning every step of the way. Nick preceded him. They stepped on the porch.

'What are you gonna do with your prisoner, Boss? Are you gonna sit with him all night?'

'I want to talk to him some more.' Strafford brandished the empty gun. 'Step in the house, Carter, and don't try anything. Bullard, go and get some sleep. We'll all be pretty busy in the morning.'

Nick stepped into the house, his hands shoulder high. Bullard stomped off the porch and departed. Strafford closed the door and Carter snatched the empty gun from him. Nick stared at his brother, his expression changing. Carter gave Nick the empty gun.

'It needs reloading,' he said. 'Strafford's gun belt is over there. You'd better put it on and get ready for action. It's clean up time now, or I miss my guess.'

'How'd you get here so fast?' Nick demanded.

'Never mind that now. We've got work to do. Find a rope to tie Strafford's hands. We'll take him back to the jail. He'll be more comfortable there.'

'You'll never be able to hold him.'

'Just watch me.' Carter grinned. 'We'll give this outfit time to hit the sack and then move out.'

Nick shrugged, found a length of rope, and bound Strafford's hands. He buckled Strafford's gun belt around his waist and reloaded the empty gun. Carter remained alert, but was impatient to get moving. When he felt that enough time had elapsed he went to the door and opened it a crack and spent some time looking out at the yard.

'I'll fetch two horses, one for Strafford and one for you, Nick. Keep an eye on him. I don't want him getting away from you.'

He slipped out to the porch, his pistol ready in his right hand. He placed his back against the front wall of the house and studied the yard; certain there would be at least one guard on duty. He was about to go on to the corral when he saw the faint red glow of a cigarette over by the cook shack close to the bunk house. He left the porch instantly and began to stalk the guard. When he reached a corner of the cook shack, the guard had already entered and a lamp was burning dimly inside.

Carter eased open the door of the building and moved inside. The guard was seated at a table, a cup of coffee in front of him. He did not know Carter was there until the muzzle of Carter's gun prodded the side of his neck. He froze instantly.

'Is anyone else wandering around the spread besides you?' Carter asked.

The man shook his head, physically incapable of answering. His eyes were bulging with shock. Carter disarmed him, saw a lariat hanging from a hook on the wall, and used it to bind him.

'I shall be on the ranch for quite some time,' Carter told him, 'and if I hear any noise coming from here I'll come back in and shoot you.'

He departed and went to the nearby tack room, found Strafford's large, ornate saddle and took it with other gear and put it on the top bar of the corral. He went back for saddle gear for a second horse and picked up a lariat. He went to the corral, where a score of horses was standing, some of them

143

made restless by his presence. He ignored Strafford's white stallion, which was standing in the background, breathing hard and snorting, and threw his loop over a quieter horse. He led it outside the corral and saddled it for travel and then caught a second horse. When he was ready to leave he led the animals over to the porch.

Nick brought Strafford outside when he heard hoofs in the yard.

'Tie him in his saddle,' Carter said, and stood watching the shadows until Nick had obeyed. Star shine had turned the darkness into a silvery, ghostly light that enabled them to see objects but suffused the scenery with deception. But Carter was looking for movement, and everywhere was still.

'We're ready to ride,' Nick said, swinging into his saddle.

'Go on ahead and I'll follow. I'll keep an eye on our rear.'

The ride back to town was without incident and, when they reached the main street, Nick rode straight to the law office. There was lamplight inside the office, and Carter drew his pistol as he dismounted at the edge of the sidewalk. Nick busied himself untying Strafford and stuck a gun muzzle against the rancher's spine. Carter tried the door of the law office, found it was locked, and tapped on it with the muzzle of his pistol.

'Who's out there?' a harsh voice demanded.

'I've got a prisoner,' Carter replied. 'Open the door.'

A key grated in the lock and the door swung open. Carter saw Deputy Swanson peering out at him.

'I thought you'd be in the next county by now,' said Carter, sticking his gun into Swanson's big belly. He snatched the pistol from the deputy's holster and crowded forward, compelling Swanson to step back into the office. 'Where's Haskell?' he demanded.

'He ain't in town right now. He said he'd be back tomorrow. He had a report of rustling on the range and has gone to check it out.'

'That's more than he did when I came in to report missing stock,' Nick said. 'All I got was a visit by someone who shot at me.'

'Are you hinting that it might have been me?' Swanson demanded.

'I know who it was – Strafford's top gun, Larkin, and I'm looking forward to the day I can draw a bead on him.' Nick pushed Strafford into the office, entered and closed the door. 'Ain't that right, Strafford? You know all about it, because you gave Larkin his orders.'

'I don't know what you're taking about,' Strafford retorted.

'You're the one who's after my spread. You thought I'd be finished by now, but now the cows are coming home to be counted, and we're getting the rights of it. Shall I put Strafford in a cell, Link?'

'Sure, and while you're at it put Swanson in a cell, lock the door, and throw away the key. Then we'll get down to working out what we should do next.'

'That's easy,' Nick asserted. 'I'd like to know all about the bank robbery, considering I was supposed to be one of the robbers.'

'Do we have any prisoners in the cells?' Carter asked Swanson.

The big deputy shrugged. 'It's empty back there,' he admitted. 'They got loose when the lynch party showed up.'

'Larkin, too?' Carter shook his head. 'Stick these two in cells, Nick. You hold the fort here and I'll pay a visit to Maddock. That banker has got some explaining to do.'

Nick took the cell keys off Swanson and urged the two prisoners into the cell block. He smiled as he turned the key.

Nick stood in the doorway, watching him. 'We need a couple of reliable men to take over in here,' he said. 'If we don't, someone will let the prisoners out the minute we turn our backs.'

'We'll do something about that later,' Carter told him. 'Right now, I want Maddock back behind bars. I'll go pick him up, and you stay here to mind the office. This time make sure all the doors are locked and you're ready for callers.'

'I won't get caught again,' Nick promised.

'Where will I find Maddock at this time of the day?' Carter asked.

'He lives in a big house at the south end of the street, where the top folks live. He's got a two-storey house on the left-hand side of the street as you go left out of here. It's the second house in the row.'

'I'll find him.' Carter departed again and went rapidly along the street. Darkness was now complete, and he dropped his right hand to the butt of his holstered gun. His nerves were steady, his eyes keen on his surroundings.

No lights were shining in Maddock's house. Carter walked around the place, looking in all the lower windows. The house had an air of desertion about it. He stepped back and checked the upper windows for lamplight, with the same result. Maddock was not at home. But that was reasonable, Carter thought. Maddock had been exposed as a criminal, so he had either fled from the town or was preparing to do so. He decided to visit Art Forder at the saloon. Maddock would not just up and leave at a moment's notice. He had crooked friends in town, and someone must know his whereabouts.

He retraced his steps to the saloon and, when he peered over the batwings, the first man he saw was Strafford's top gunman, Larkin, standing at the bar with a tot of whiskey before him. He was alone and fully armed, Carter noticed. He watched Larkin for several moments, trying to decide whether to arrest him or take him later, and the fact that Larkin would draw a gun on him the moment they met gave Carter no option. He loosened his pistol in its holster and pushed through the batwings.

Larkin saw him immediately with the aid of the back-bar mirror, and his reaction was instant and fast.

147

He drew his right-hand gun and turned at bay, like a wounded cougar. Carter went along with the action, reaching for his gun and cocking it. He was covering Larkin as the gunman tightened his finger on his trigger. But Carter fired first, and the silence of the saloon was broken with the noise of gun thunder. Larkin was coming forward, but he found it too difficult to control his pistol with Carter's .45 slug in his chest. He fell against the man at his side and they both dropped to the floor.

The saloon room froze as the shot hammered. All heads turned to focus on the shoot-out. The man who had been knocked down by Larkin's fall scrambled to his feet and backed away with his hands half raised to show they were empty, and the sound of footsteps coming along the bar warned Carter that Art Forder was on his way towards him.

'You'll give this place a bad name,' Forder said angrily.

'You're not out of the wood yet.' Carter's words stopped Forder in mid flow. His expression changed, and he fell silent and waited for Carter to say more.

'You should bar killers from your saloon,' Carter replied. 'Larkin murdered three of my brother's crew out at the ranch – shot them down in cold blood. I had arrested him, but he got out when the lynch party showed up.'

'None of that has got anything to do with me.' A plaintive note sounded in Forder's tone. 'I'm running an honest business here.'

148

'Where's Cassie?' Carter demanded.

'She's in her room. She's due to sing in a few moments. Do you want to see her?'

'I want to ask her some questions.'

'Leave it until after she's sung her next song.'

'Are you afraid I might ask something that will upset her?'

'She hasn't put a foot wrong in the time I've known her,' Forder rapped.

'So, you've forgotten Texas already, huh?' Carter smiled. 'Get her out here now and I'll talk to her. If her answers are not to my liking, then she won't get the chance to sing her next song – she'll be behind bars.'

'There must be some mistake!' Forder's face turned a grey shade of ash. 'You can't do this, Carter.'

'Who is gonna stop me?'

Forder glanced quickly around the saloon, a hint of fear in his eyes.

'I'll fetch her,' he said.

'I'll go with you,' Carter replied. 'You lead the way.'

Forder shrugged and walked to the rear of the saloon. Carter stayed at his left shoulder. They entered the door of the office, and Forder opened an inner door to reveal Cassie seated at a dressing table in front of a large mirror. She frowned at their interruption, until she recognized Carter, and then she forced a smile, which faltered, and made an effort to renew it.

'Carter insists on seeing you now, Cassie,' Forder said.

She glanced at a clock on the wall and shook her head.

'Can't it wait until after my song?'

'I'm afraid not.' Carter shook his head. 'It's only a short question but be careful how you answer it because I've got a witness that remembers exactly what you said, and he's prepared to stand up in court and repeat your words.'

'Let's have the question,' said Forder impatiently.

'Cassie saw Frank Bullard, Strafford's ranch foreman, earlier at the livery barn. She talked to him as if they were old friends and had a message for him to pass to Strafford. She said Strafford should ease off grabbing range because his actions were causing trouble for the main game.'

Forder opened his mouth to speak but Carter's glance warned him to remain silent.

'Let me hear what Cassie has to say before you jump in with both feet, Forder. If she can't answer to my satisfaction, then you'll both be behind bars.'

'I have no idea what you are talking about,' Cassie snapped. She glanced at Forder with sudden appeal in her eyes, hoping for his guidance, and compressed her lips when he remained silent.

'This is ridiculous,' said Forder eventually.

Carter struck him with a heavy right-hand punch. Forder yelped sharply in pain and dropped to the floor on his hands and knees.

'I told you to keep quiet,' Carter looked at Cassie. She seemed as if the floor had opened suddenly at her feet and she was teetering on the edge of a precipice. 'Do you deny seeing Frank Bullard at the livery barn?'

'I saw him.' She passed a hand wearily across her pale forehead. 'I happened to be passing the barn and he spoke to me. He's not a stranger to me. We were friends a long, long time ago.'

'What did you say to him?'

She shook her head uncertainly. 'I really can't remember.'

'It was a message that Forder asked you to pass on. You didn't meet Bullard by chance. You went to find him. So, what was the message? If you persist in saying you can't recall it, then I'll have to jail you until you can remember. I think you're holding out on me.'

'How do you know I spoke to Bullard today?'

'You don't need to know that. You're on the hook and the best thing you can do is come clean.'

She glanced at Forder, who was trying to get up off the floor, and then looked into Carter's eyes.

'I'm not mixed up in anything. I told Forder after what happened in Texas when you ran us out of town that I would never get involved in his schemes again.'

Carter nodded. 'So, you're clean but he's still on that old trail, huh? Why don't you open up, Cassie, and tell me what's going on? If you're innocent then you'll be able to walk away from this, free as a bird.'

Forder managed to get into a sitting position, and he was half-turned away from Carter, his right hand sliding inside his jacket, reaching into his left armpit. Carter watched him until the hand reappeared from the jacket, saw that it was holding a gun, and lunged forward to grapple with him. While he was concentrating on Forder, Cassie lifted a .41 derringer from under a cloth on the table and turned on Carter, her face contorted with deadly intention.

She fired the pistol. The crash of the shot filled the small room with gun thunder. Carter felt the impact of the slug as if he had been struck by lightning. Pain stabbed through him, although momentarily, he had no idea where he was hit. His sense of balance fled and he became aware that the floor was coming up to smack him in the face. He lost consciousness. . . .

ELEVEN

Carter came back to his senses with a strong hand shaking him. He tried to get away from the hand, for pain was swirling up from his right side above the hip, threatening to overwhelm him. He opened his eyes and saw Rough Milligan on one knee beside him, holding a gun and pointing it at someone out of Carter's line of sight. Carter lifted his head and saw Forder and Cassie across the room with their hands raised.

'It was lucky I've been trailing you,' Milligan said. 'I was outside the batwings when you killed Larkin, and I sneaked into the saloon when you came in here with Forder. I was outside this door when I heard a shot, and when I came in you looked like you were dead.'

Carter made an effort to sit up, but pain stabbed through his side and he slumped back.

'Take a look at me and check my wound,' he said through gritted teeth. 'It feels as if a rib is busted.'

'You've got a big bruise on your forehead,' Milligan observed. He looked at Cassie. 'You shot him, so get over here and take a look at his wound.'

'Get the doctor in,' she replied harshly. 'He's gonna put us behind bars when he's on his feet.'

'You better believe it.' Carter sat up again, grasped Milligan's left arm and dragged himself to his feet. He leaned heavily on the big man and turned his attention to Forder. 'So you gave Cassie a message for Bullard, and she can't remember what it was. Don't tell me you've forgotten it as well, Forder.'

'That's right,' said Forder, smiling weakly. 'Say, you'd better get to the doctor quick. You look like you're ready to drop.'

Carter glanced at Milligan, who was eyeing Forder like he was something that had crawled out of a hole in the ground.

'I ain't up to handling Forder at the moment,' Carter said, 'so perhaps you'll attend to him.'

'It'll be my pleasure.' Milligan grinned and moved in like a mad dog. The big man struck Forder with a clenched fist that sent him backwards on his heels until he slammed into a wall. The back of Forder's head hit the wall and he fell to the floor. Milligan bent over him, dragged him back on his feet, and hit him with a series of left and right blows that dropped him senseless at Carter's feet.

'That'll do for the moment,' said Carter as Milligan started to drag Forder upright.

Milligan stepped backwards, grinning.

'Throw some water over him,' Carter said, and Milligan looked around, saw a large jug of water standing on a table, and picked it up.

Forder gasped as the water struck him. He gasped and opened his eyes. Carter moved to a chair and sat down heavily.

'Get him on his feet, Milligan. Let's give him a chance to speak.'

Milligan lifted Forder and supported him as he sagged and began to slip to the floor again.

'What was the message you gave Cassie for Bullard?' Carter demanded.

'You can't do this,' Forder gasped. 'You've got no legal right. I want to see the sheriff.'

'You and me both,' Carter replied. He glanced at Milligan who was holding his pistol and gazing at Forder like a guard dog facing a trespasser. 'Let's put these two in a cell until I can get around to giving them my full attention.' He pressed his left hand against the pain in his lower right ribs, and his fingers became sticky with blood.

Milligan took charge of the prisoners and took them out the back door of the saloon with Carter following closely, his gun in his hand. They passed along an alley to the main street and kept in the shadows as they headed for the jail. Carter had to sidle along, favouring his right side, for his right leg was protesting painfully at the movement of walking. He held his gun in his left hand and pressed the inside of his right elbow into the painful area on his lower ribs, which did nothing to ease the pain.

When they reached the door of the law office, Carter remained behind Forder and Cassie. Milligan eased forward and knocked on the door. Nick answered from inside and Carter replied. Nick unlocked the door, and it was then that Carter sensed someone appearing on his left from the darkness of the alley beside the jail. A gun was jabbed into his back, and a second man appeared on his right and reached for his holster. As the office door swung open the two newcomers put their arms around Carter and Forder and thrust them against Milligan, driving all three across the threshold into the office, and following closely. Cassie screamed as she was bundled forward, and slipped and fell across the threshold, taking Carter down with her.

Milligan turned like a cat, his gun lifting. A gun crashed just above Carter's head, and Milligan rocked on his feet but continued to move. Carter saw blood spurt from Milligan's chest, but the big man bared his teeth and fired at someone beyond Carter, who heard a cry of pain, and then a heavy body fell across him and Cassie, Carter recognized Swanson's big face, contorted in pain, as the deputy rolled limply and lay dead partly across Cassie.

Another voice shouted, and Carter recognized Sheriff Haskell. He has been on Carter's right, and pushed forward into the doorway, gun in hand, and lifted the weapon to shoot Nick, who was in the act of drawing his gun. Two shots blasted almost simultaneously, and gun smoke swirled around the doorway. Nick stepped back into the office, and his gun crashed again. The sheriff dropped his gun and sprawled forward to lie across Swanson's legs.

Carter gritted his teeth and made the effort to rise. The pain in his lower ribs was excruciating but he persisted, and lumbered to his feet, reeling farther into the office as he tried to retain his balance. Nick came forward. There was blood on his left arm just above the elbow. He grabbed Carter and led him across the office and dumped him on a chair by the desk. Carter lifted his left arm; found he was still holding his pistol and levelled it at the doorway. Milligan was leaning against a doorpost, blood staining his shirt on his left side. He sat down suddenly, but still covered Forder. Cassie had stopped screaming, although her mouth remained open and she was almost out of her mind in shock.

Carter looked at Nick. 'We got two prisoners for you,' he said.

Nick laughed grimly. 'I'll take Forder and Cassie,' he replied. 'Swanson's obviously dead, and the sheriff looks as if he's on the same trail to hell.'

Carter got to his feet with difficulty and approached Milligan. Nick dragged Cassie to her feet and nudged Forder with his foot. They got up and Nick took them into the cells. Carter grasped Milligan's right arm, and the big man pitched forward into his arms. Carter lowered him to the floor. Milligan groaned and slumped, his face contorting, but he opened his eyes and looked at Carter.

'I'm OK,' he said, 'but I need the doc.'

'We'll get him as soon as we can. Hang in there.'

Sheriff Haskell groaned and moved convulsively. Nick bent over him. The sheriff was bleeding from a chest wound. His face was pallid, his breathing laboured.

'So, you made it,' gasped Haskell, looking up at Nick. 'I thought we had you hogtied to the bank robbery. Maddock was working with Strafford to clean up on the local range. It was his idea to frame you as a bank robber.'

'Where is Maddock?' Carter demanded. 'He's not at home. Has he lit out?'

Haskell closed his eyes, fighting for his breath. 'It don't matter now,' he gasped. 'It's done. We played for high stakes and lost.' His breath trailed away, and his head fell sideways. He died with a convulsive tremor.

'I'll fetch the doc,' Nick said. 'You keep an eye on the place until I get back.'

Carter nodded and moved to the seat behind the desk, placing his gun near to hand. Nick departed, leaving the door open. Carter had to try hard to remain alert, but his eyes closed despite his efforts. When he heard a footstep in the doorway he jerked upright, reaching for his pistol. He saw Maddock peering into the office, and his gun seemed heavy as a millstone as he lifted it to cover the banker.

'It's good to see you, Maddock,' Carter said. 'I've got some questions to ask you. Come on in and sit down.'

Maddock stepped around the bodies of Swanson and Haskell without looking at them. His fleshy face was haggard, and he had a hunted look, like a wolf on its last legs. Carter noted that he was at a disadvantage, sitting in a lighted room with the door open, and darkness pressing in against the big front window. He picked up his gun from the desk and started to his feet to get out of line with anyone standing outside, and even as he moved he saw a bearded face pushing close outside the window, and lamp light glinted on a pistol the man was holding.

Carter dropped to one knee and raised his gun. He saw muzzle flame outside, heard the window smash, and sensed a bullet skim the left side his face. He fired in return, and the man outside fell away. He swung to see what Maddock was doing. The banker was in the act of producing a pistol. His eyes were wide, his mouth gaping. In his nervousness he fumbled the gun, almost dropped it, and Carter thumbed back his hammer. Maddock tried to hurry his movement, but he was no match for Carter. He cried out in fear when he realized that Carter would get off his shot first and screwed up his fleshy face in anticipation. When the shot came, the bullet punched into his shoulder, the impact causing his gun to fall from his hand. He fell backwards and lay motionless, his eyes closed tightly.

Carter's pistol dropped out of his grasp onto the desk and he went back to sit in the chair, aware that Maddock was the last man he needed. He'd had no intention of killing the banker. His testimony would be invaluable. Relief filled him when he realized that the shooting was over. He was feeling extremely tired, and his strength seem to flow out of him like water running out of a busted can. Darkness was hovering around the periphery of his sight, threatening to move in and overwhelm him if he did not relax, and he suddenly realized that it really was all over. He had beaten the bad men, and all that remained was the task of sorting out who was guilty of what. . . .